Jack was there with her son.
Their son. *His* son.

Kevin was trying not to stare at the brown bag Jack had sitting on his lap.

"Don't you want to know who the surprise is for?" Jack asked, his attention on Kevin.

He'd make a wonderful father. The unexpected thought caught Erica completely off guard. In another time, another life, Jack would've been able to give so much. On the few occasions she'd seen him with Kevin, she'd noticed the natural affinity he seemed to have with children.

Or was it just *his* son?

Was she robbing them both of something vital by keeping her secret? In trying to protect them was she hurting them instead? Inflicting more pain where she tried so hard to bring happiness?

Or would telling her secret cause the greater pain?

And what about Jefferson, the man Kevin called Daddy? He might be her ex-husband but he considered Kevin his son.

"So who's the surprise for?" Kevin's voice rose on the last word as he stared at the bag.

"I think it's for you," Jack said.

Dear Reader,

The book you're holding is very special to me. This is a story about love—in its purest form—in the hands and hearts of human beings who are not perfect. It probably isn't the type of love story you find very often in a romance novel, yet it epitomizes everything that reading Harlequin books while I was growing up taught me about love and life. About the possibilities awaiting me. About the things I could hope for. Things I'd find only if I lived my life heroically. If I strove always to be a good person and make the right choices.

I grew up believing in the love I now write about. And then, clinging diligently to those beliefs, I flung myself out into the world where good and bad weren't so clearly delineated, where the right choices weren't always obvious. Where the heart could be confused.

I discovered something miraculous. The love we read about and come back to time and time again, the hope, the assurance that, in the end, right wins—it's all true. It's not as easy as it looked in the books I grew up reading, though. Finding that happy ending takes the ability to endure, to forgive oneself for not being perfect, to strive—especially in the face of mistakes—to do what's right. To never stop believing you can be a good person.

So this story is for all the people like me who have the courage to live in this world full of bumps and bruises and still believe.

Please approach Erica, Jack, Jefferson, Pamela and Kevin with an open heart. I'm confident they'll do the rest....

Sincerely,

Tara Taylor Quinn

P.S. I love hearing from readers. Write me at P.O. Box 15065, Scottsdale, AZ 85267 or visit me at www.tarataylorquinn.com.

The _Secret_ Son
Tara Taylor Quinn

HARLEQUIN®

TORONTO • NEW YORK • LONDON
AMSTERDAM • PARIS • SYDNEY • HAMBURG
STOCKHOLM • ATHENS • TOKYO • MILAN • MADRID
PRAGUE • WARSAW • BUDAPEST • AUCKLAND

ISBN 0-373-71057-7

THE SECRET SON

Copyright © 2002 by Tara Lee Reames.

Visit us at www.eHarlequin.com

Printed in U.S.A.

DEDICATION

For Kevin. This is the great thing about being a writer. What you can't have, you can create. Since the first day we met—and I fell in love—I've had a great yearning in my heart to have known you as a little boy....

And

For Jake Bodell. I'm fairly certain you wouldn't read this book in a million years, or like it if you did (except for the setting and the political parts). But it was you and your ability to act upon promptings that provided me with the strength to get it written. You are an amazing young man.

ACKNOWLEDGMENT

All the dog jokes contained herein are the property of scatty.com (www.scatty.com), whom the author wishes to thank for their generosity in allowing her to use them.

CHAPTER ONE

September 1996

IT HAD BEEN thc best—and the worst   week of her life.

Walking up Fifth Avenue, Erica was barely aware of the Thursday-afternoon crowd pressing around her. Years ago crowds had bothered her. Not anymore.

Going home to face Jefferson, now *that* was going to be horrible. To look into those loving gray eyes and know she'd betrayed him...

Oh, not physically. She could give herself that much credit. Sort of. In the past week she'd kissed Jack. Touched him. Let him touch her.

Okay, begged for his touch.

But they hadn't made love.

Thinking of Jefferson, that was a huge comfort; thinking of Jack, of never seeing him again, of never knowing what it would feel like to be held, to be loved, by the man who'd awakened her heart fully for the first time in her life, there was no comfort at all. That knowledge brought such incredible grief she could hardly breathe.

But it had to be that way. She was a married woman.

And Jack, a former FBI agent, was a freelance hostage negotiator, always on call, ready to run at a moment's notice, married to his job. A job, he'd told her, that he wouldn't be able to do if he had someone waiting at home for him. A job filled with risks he wouldn't be able to take if he had someone relying on him.

They'd spent this one stolen, enchanting week in New York City while he waited for the call to move and she was getting the runaround from a *Wall Street Journal* reporter she'd come to straighten out about Jefferson's public support of stem-cell research. If it hadn't been for the threat of some very real damage to Senator Jefferson Cooley's reputation because of the bad—and worse, inaccurate—press coverage he'd received from the *Journal,* his communications director would not have had to risk her emotional health by staying in the city all those days. As soon as she'd met Jack Shaw she'd have hightailed it back to Washington.

To her husband.

And boss.

A man who was twenty-seven years her senior.

When she'd finally spoken with the reporter an hour ago, he'd promised a retraction. And another article, telling the real story. The story Erica had written herself and handed him as she left the meeting.

She could escape New York. And the temptation of Jack.

Her flight left JFK at seven the next morning, putting her in Washington in time to make the morning staff meeting at the senator's office.

She'd have liked to go tonight. To make it home in time to crawl into bed beside him and tell herself she'd done him no wrong.

Maggie's Place. It was the pub where she and Jack had first met. They'd both enjoyed the place, with its long mahogany bar and Irish charm, and they'd gone there every night for the past six nights. And stayed until closing.

It had been on one of the tables set for two along the side wall of the pub that Jack's fingers had found hers. And clung. They'd been talking about their favorite television sitcoms at the time.

Shaking her stylishly cropped head of short dark hair, Erica still couldn't understand why she hadn't carefully pulled her hand free. Or why she'd gone back the next night.

When she'd married Jefferson three years before, she'd promised him loyalty.

He'd known she wasn't in love with him.

A longtime friend of her family's, he'd been one of the guests at her wedding to Shane. She'd been a naive, idealistic twenty-two.

Four years later he'd been there to help Erica pick up the pieces when that marriage ended. She was already working in his office by then, Congress had been in session, and he'd given her very little time off, insisting that work was what would see her through.

He'd been right.

As he almost always was.

He'd told her, one night when he'd come into the office late and found her crying over the writing of what should have been a simple speech, that the happiest years of her life weren't behind her. That eventually she'd love again.

She'd refused to believe him.

Jefferson had shaken his head, telling her to give it some time.

But love hadn't come to her a second time, and after Shane, it never would. Or so she'd thought until this past week.

The possibility that Jefferson might have been right—and that she'd found out several years too late—scared her to death.

Until this week she'd consoled herself with the thought that she'd already endured the worst life had to offer. That nothing she had yet to face would be harder than surviving Shane's betrayal.

She'd been wrong.

Leaving Jack was going to be worse. Far worse.

Walking around the corner to Forty-seventh Street, Erica could see Maggie's Place just ahead. She'd been telling herself all day that she wasn't going to the pub that night. Jack had given her a quick goodnight kiss the night before. The affectionate kind of kiss shared by friends.

And she'd felt it all the way to her toes.

Jack was danger. Making her want things—believe in things—she couldn't have. She was better off not knowing they existed. She had to stay away from him.

Her feet carried her toward the pub, anyway.

Jack risked his life whenever he went to work. He walked into highly volatile situations to save the lives of strangers, negotiating with madmen and extremists and desperate people who had nothing to lose. He'd told her she was the first person he'd connected with on a personal level in more than five years.

She couldn't just leave him sitting there. Couldn't go without thanking him for giving back to her what Shane had stripped from her all those years ago. Her belief in herself—and in a chemistry that made life exciting. In possibilities.

She couldn't go without telling him goodbye.

Jefferson had her life. She could at least give Jack goodbye.

He was sitting at "their" table. The one halfway down the row. "You look beautiful," he told her, smiling, his eyes warm with seductive appreciation as she pulled out her chair.

She'd worn the black ankle-length pants and red blouse more for him than for the *Journal* reporter.

"Thank you," she said, her trepidation disappearing as she took her seat across from him.

In this city where anyone could get lost in the crowd, her time with him existed in a universe all its own.

It seemed to Erica that being with Jack brought her face-to-face with the person inside herself, the person she really was. How could anything that felt this natural, this *destined*, be wrong?

He was wearing jeans and a black polo shirt that

hugged his chest, the bands at the bottoms of the short sleeves tight around his biceps.

"Did you get your call?" she asked, although it made no difference.

Hours were all they had left. They'd both known that from the beginning.

"Did you have your meeting?" he countered, glancing down into his beer.

He hadn't answered her question.

Erica waited until he looked up, his beautiful eyes meeting hers, before she nodded.

In his gaze she saw a flash of the same desperate sadness she felt herself.

"When are you leaving?" he asked.

"In the morning. I have a seven o'clock out of JFK."

"I go in the morning, too."

Although it made no sense at all, disappointment crashed through her.

"Where?" she asked, telling herself not to be afraid for him.

"Florida."

A teenage boy was being held hostage by a suspected drug dealer who wanted safe passage to Cuba. The FBI Crisis Negotiation chief had called Jack earlier in the week to speak with him about the situation. They'd still been searching for the boy at that point.

"The hostage-taker's ready to negotiate?" she murmured.

Jack nodded.

"So why do *you* have to go?" She cringed, hoping

that didn't sound as bad to Jack's ears as it had to hers.

"I speak the language, for one thing. The guy's Latin American."

"You can't be the only one."

He took a sip of his beer, studying the suds. "A few years ago I had a successful negotiation involving him. He's agreed to talk, under the stipulation that I be the one he speaks to."

"He's taken hostages before?"

"No." Jack shook his head, frowning. "He *was* a hostage."

"Oh!" Taken aback, Erica studied him.

And she'd thought *she* had a tough job.

"So—" he looked across at her, his weathered face solemn "—tonight's it, then."

"Yeah."

His hand was close to hers on the table. Just the smallest movement would bring their fingers together again.

"Maybe we should go upstairs to the dining room or something as a sort of send-off."

"I'd rather stay right here." Where they'd spent every minute they'd ever had together.

He sat back, his hand sliding off the table. "I'm glad we had this week," he said.

"I am, too." The words were almost a whisper. Her throat hurt with the effort to get them out at all.

How was she going to live the rest of her life without ever seeing him again?

He finished his beer and motioned for another.

"Knowing that you're in the world gives my life a whole new dimension," he said quietly.

She couldn't speak, afraid of what might spill forth, afraid of the regrets she'd have to face when she left their world and returned to her own.

"It's something we can take with us," he added.

Erica tried to smile. "Thank you for that."

"Hey." He leaned forward, his thumb following a path down her cheek. "We have hours yet." His face was softly lit with a half smile that almost made her cry. "Let's not lose them."

Her face, her entire body, responding to the light touch of his thumb, Erica nodded.

"I think pita pizzas are in order."

It was their favorite of Maggie's munchies. They'd tried them all.

Erica forced a grin and determined that she'd make the next hours the absolute best they could be.

By the time the pizza arrived, she'd just about managed to pretend that this was like any other night that week—a beginning, instead of the end.

Except for the underlying desperation. Now when they talked, they didn't hesitate before they jumped into any topic. If they only had this one night, they didn't have time for deliberation, for careful phrasing or circumspect questions.

Erica couldn't take her gaze off him, even for a second, frightened of losing the chance to store up one more memory. He seemed to be having the same problem, his eyes more intent—though she wouldn't have believed that possible—than they'd been all those other nights.

They were drinking faster.

Eating faster.

They were doing everything faster, speeding through years of their lives, trying to squeeze in every single memory.

And then, suddenly, they stopped. The noise in the pub continued around them—the murmur of conversation, intermittent laughter, the clinking of glasses— but Erica and Jack were surrounded by silence.

Emotions engulfed her. Confused her. There was so much, so many feelings. And yet not nearly enough.

"Why do you have to be a hostage negotiator?" she blurted out, terrified for his safety, although it wasn't her business to be.

Shaking his head, he took a protracted swig of beer. And then he said, "I was married once. A long time ago."

Erica's stomach tensed. "You didn't tell me that."

"I know." Both hands grasped the cold mug, and he didn't meet her eyes, gazing someplace over her shoulder, instead.

"I'd just joined the agency," he finally began. "Completed my training. She was a flight attendant. We'd met in college."

"She went to college to be a flight attendant?"

"Melissa had a degree in education. Loved kids, hated teaching." Jack's tone of voice, the faraway look in his eyes, testified that he'd loved his wife.

"She liked flying?"

"She liked traveling, and I was gone a lot."

"So what happened?"

He glanced back at Erica and some of his tension—the stiffness in his shoulders, the whiteness of his knuckles around that mug—dissipated. "She got pregnant. We'd been married a little over three years and were both ready...."

Pregnant. Jack had a child.

Erica was finding it difficult to breathe, but she listened anyway, feeling his love for his family—sensing his pain.

When he reached across and took her hand, holding it with both of his, it was the most natural thing in the world. His palms felt cold from the mug of beer.

"We had a girl, Courtney Marie...."

Jack swallowed with apparent difficulty. His eyes had a definite sheen.

"When she was a couple of months old, Melissa took Courtney to see her mother out in California. My mother-in-law taught at a high school in Malibu, and Melissa went to meet her for lunch one day."

He paused again. Erica squeezed his hand, holding on.

"A couple of kids went crazy, pulled guns out of their backpacks, started yelling."

"Oh, my God," Erica whispered. "Jack, don't. You don't have to do this."

"According to the reports, it was all pretty chaotic after that. Some random shots were fired, but apparently no one was hurt. Officials started closing in on the kids. They got scared. And around the corner walked Melissa with Courtney in a carrier on her chest...."

Erica, seeing the story's end, swallowed back tears.

"One of the kids grabbed her, held her in front of him while he made his way out of the school. They were holed up in his van for more than three hours before gunshots were heard again. When the authorities got inside the van, Melissa and Courtney had been killed by a single shot. I was working here in New York and they couldn't reach me."

"What happened to the kid?" It didn't matter. Erica didn't give a damn about the kid. She just had to get her mind off that young woman and her baby.

Jack's baby.

"He was dead, too."

Jack's eyes were bleak. Vacant. And completely dry.

Erica had to fight not to cry for him.

"Jack," she said, attempting to bring him back to her if she could. "I'm sorry. So incredibly sorry."

As he refocused on her, Erica could see the raging emotions he was struggling to control. "I know," he said.

There was nothing she could do for him, nothing she could say that was going to make any difference at all to the despair he was fighting. She could only sit there. Give him her love. And hope that there really was some healing power in a human heart.

"She was only two months old. Not even rolling over yet." His voice was low. "That's when I joined the Crisis Negotiation team."

Erica ached to hold him in her arms.

She ached for a lot of things she couldn't have.

CHAPTER TWO

HOURS PASSED. Erica drank four more glasses of wine, well past her limit. But without the numbness it brought, she'd never be able to walk away from Jack and go home to the man she'd married.

Maggie's was closing within the hour. There were only a few late-night stragglers left.

"I'm glad Jefferson is good to you."

"I don't deserve his goodness," Erica said. She'd always felt that way, but never more so than she did at this moment, sitting here with Jack, clutching his hand, afraid that she'd fallen in love with him.

"How can you say that?" Jack argued. "You spend your life presenting him in the best possible light, giving everything you have to the building of his reputation."

"He's in love with me."

"I sure as hell hope so." The words were sharp.

"I love him, too, but I'm not *in* love with him."

"You said he knew that going in."

She nodded. "I'd been working in his office for several years, and I'd recently received the promotion to communications director." Erica, remembering back three years before, could hardly make sense of decisions that had seemed so logical and clear-cut. "The Republican senatorial race in Massachusetts was going to be brutal that year. While Jefferson's reputation was good, so was the reputation of the state prosecutor hoping to win his seat. No matter how much we pumped the issues, the campaign was going to come down to the fact that the prosecutor had a beautiful wife and three honor-student kids, and Jefferson was childless and had been divorced for several years."

She didn't want to waste precious time talking about this. And yet, it was important to know he understood.

She stared at their hands. His tanned skin was in stark contrast to her paleness. She loved the back of his hand, covered with a sprinkling of the same sandy hair that fell across his forehead.

His touch was bittersweet, promising things she'd stopped believing in.

"One night, late, after consuming almost an entire bottle of wine to unwind from a particularly grueling week, Jefferson confessed that he'd been in love with me for years."

It was well past midnight now. Their hours had turned into minutes.

Jack's eyes narrowed. "He just blurted it out?"

"No." She shook her head. "That's not Jefferson's style. He was arguing with me, actually, disputing a statement I'd just made about the nonexistence of love. I told him the emotion was a fantasy.

That its power was ephemeral. That the happiness I thought I'd found with Shane didn't really exist.''

It had been one of her many misconceptions, though she hadn't discovered that until this past week.

"We debated through another glass of wine, and then I finally just told him that if love did exist, it wasn't anything I was going to allow in my life again. I refused to be that vulnerable. Wasn't going to give someone else the power to hurt me that much.''

"A wise decision.''

Erica wasn't surprised he agreed. After sharing a sardonic grin with him, she continued. "At that point, with the conversation at a standstill and the bottle of wine gone, Jefferson's confession lay between us like…like some shocking indiscretion.''

The bartender came over and handed Jack their final tab. Without letting go of her hand, he fumbled with his wallet, threw his credit card on the table. He caressed her palm with his fingers—and the rest of her with his eyes.

Time was almost up.

She needed more to drink. She wasn't numb enough yet.

"What happened next?'' he asked, as though their world wasn't coming to an end.

"We talked awkwardly about the campaign for a few minutes, trying to get back on familiar ground. The talk came around to Jefferson's single status, and the solution seemed obvious. We should get married. He must've asked me fifteen times if I was sure I didn't harbor some secret dream about a knight in shining armor.

"I pointed out that I hadn't had a date since my divorce and that I didn't want one.

"He said he hated the thought of me living my whole life alone. I told him I wasn't thrilled with the idea myself, but that it was far better than the alternative.

"He asked me to marry him and eventually I accepted."

The bartender came back with the receipt for Jack to sign. Resentment shot through Erica. Couldn't the man have given them a few more minutes?

"Two months later we were married, and four months after that, he won." She continued telling her story as though they hadn't been interrupted, as though they weren't supposed to be standing up, heading toward the door, leaving the pub.

And each other.

"I had a lot of reservations because I knew he was in love with me and I couldn't return those feelings. But in the end, he somehow convinced me that being allowed to share my life would make him happy. I let him convince me it would be enough."

The biggest mistake of all.

Jack was frowning.

"You have to understand," Erica said quickly. "It wasn't that I didn't love him. I did—I do. It's just not a stars-in-your-eyes, heartjumping kind of love. He'd been a colleague of my father's, a friend of the family for years. I'd actually had a crush on him for a short time while I was in high school.''

''Just how old is he?'' Jack asked, pulling her up to stand with him, still not relinquishing his hold on her hand.

She didn't want to tell him. Jefferson looked younger than he was, and Jack had told her he wasn't really up on Washington politicians, anyway. She was pretty sure he'd missed the publicity about her marriage to Jefferson three years before.

''Fifty-nine,'' she said with obvious reluctance.

He stopped. Stared at her. ''Twenty-seven years older than you?''

He was good with the math.

Erica nodded.

''And here I've been picturing you with some hot-shot young stud tearing up Capitol Hill. This kind of reminds me of that song by the Eagles. 'Lyin' Eyes.'''

Hand in hand, they walked to the door.

''Except that I've never visited the cheatin' side of town.''

The New York air was crisp. Cool. Forty-seventh Street was almost deserted. With the minutes closing in on her, Erica felt caged, claustrophobic.

''Let me walk you to your hotel?''

''Of course.''

But there was no ''of course'' about it. Always

before, he'd hailed her a cab on Fifth Avenue and wished her good-night.

A twenty-minute walk to her hotel—if they took things slowly—and then her soul mate was going to walk out of her life forever. How could she possibly make it through a lifetime of never feeling this way again? Of never feeling the intensity, the *rightness,* she felt when she was with Jack?

This wasn't the youthful passionate love she'd felt for Shane. It went deeper than that. Deeper than what she'd known as love.

Jack made her feel complete.

THEY WERE NEARING her hotel. Jack spent the last couple of blocks wondering whether he dared to kiss her good-night.

He was going to have to leave her without doing what he needed most—take her to bed. He didn't even question that.

Jack didn't sleep with married women.

And she wasn't the type to cheat.

Jefferson Cooley might not have passionate love from her, but he had her loyalty. And of the two, loyalty won out.

As he believed it should.

"See that guy over there?" Erica said, gesturing as they approached her hotel.

A man, dressed casually in a pair of well-fitting jeans and a button-down shirt with the sleeves rolled up, leaned against the corner of the building.

"Yeah."

"My first night here, he tried to get me to go with him, supposedly to pick out some earrings for his mother. I had to tell him no three times before he finally gave up," she said, her voice not quite steady, though from wine, their imminent goodbye or something else he couldn't be sure. "He's been hanging around the hotel all week."

She slowed her steps until they were barely moving forward at all. "For a while I thought he was out here smoking, but I've never seen him light up. A couple of times since that first night, I've caught him watching me. And then last evening, I'm almost certain he followed me into the hotel. He came in right after I did. I slipped into an elevator just as the door was closing and lost him."

Once a cop, always a cop. Jack checked the man out. Erica was right. He was watching them. Or rather, her. The guy hadn't been hanging around *his* place all week.

"I'm walking you inside," Jack said brusquely, putting an arm around Erica to lead her through the front door of the hotel.

He glared at the guy as they passed, warning him off in no uncertain terms. The other man shrugged and looked away.

The man might be perfectly harmless. Just a hotel guest appreciating a beautiful fellow guest.

But Jack had learned the hard way that you could never be sure.

Glancing back as they entered the hotel, Jack wasn't pleased to see the man still leaning there, still watching them.

It was odd, the way he'd been leaning against that wall all week. *Was* he a threat to Erica? And if so, why?

"I'd feel a whole lot better if you'd just let me see you safely up to your room."

Erica looked at him uncertainly, lightly chewing her lower lip, and he knew it wasn't just the man loitering outside that was troubling her. With every moment they prolonged this goodbye, they were giving temptation the edge, challenging a strength that might not be able to sustain them.

She nodded, silently leading the way.

Not another word was said as they rode the deserted elevator up to the twelfth floor. She paused outside a double door about halfway down the hall.

A suite. At least Jefferson Cooley kept her in style.

She slid her electronic entry card into the slot above the door handle. "I can't do this," she said suddenly, resting her head against the door.

Jack reached for the card with shaking fingers. "Here, let me."

But the green light was already on. She'd unlocked the door.

Erica turned, her eyes bright with unshed tears as she looked up at him. "I can't just go in there and leave you when I still have another six hours before I have to be at the airport...."

"What are you saying?"

"I just wish we could go somewhere and talk."

He had to work tomorrow. Lives were at stake. He had to be sharp, decisive, alert to every nuance.

But he'd have a long plane ride to recover from a sleepless night....

"It does seem criminal to waste six perfectly good hours," he said.

"We could go to that place we passed a few blocks back, the one with the yellow and green lights," she said.

Jack thought of the man hanging around outside. "I'd rather you didn't leave the hotel again, not while that guy's still down there. He's probably harmless, but just in case..."

Erica frowned, her dark-brown eyes filled with so many conflicting emotions he couldn't decipher. "Nothing in the hotel will be open this late."

Temptation battled resolve with no clear victor.

Jack took a steadying breath. At the agency, they called him a man of steel. They joked that his middle name was self-control. And it was true. A hostage negotiator had to be cool under pressure.

He reached around her to open the door of her suite. "I'll bet you have a fully stocked bar in here," he guessed, "and a perfectly good table and chairs we can use."

He glanced around the corner of the entryway. He'd been right. The bar was along the far wall. The table was glass, with four chairs around it and a big bowl of fresh fruit in the center.

"We'll pretend we're in the bar down the street, the one with the yellow and green lights, but I'll know you're safe."

She looked as though she was going to refuse. As though she *had* to refuse. And then she smiled at him.

"Okay," she said, hesitation in every line of her body. She stood there, tall, model-slim, arms tight against her sides. And he realized that if this was a risk for him, it was a greater one for her. "We're in a bar. And we have the whole night ahead of us...."

Jack wasn't sure how many shots of whiskey he consumed over the next couple of hours. He only knew that he was ahead of her and her glasses of wine probably two to one. And that it still wasn't enough.

On his last trip back from the bathroom, he couldn't make himself return to that hard wicker chair, squeezing his long legs under the ridiculous glass table. He'd been afraid something was going to break every time he set his drink down.

He wasn't sure why he'd thought staying in her suite had been such a good idea, either.

He'd miscalculated the danger. It wasn't the man outside she had to worry about but the one sitting here in her room.

She'd gone to the second bathroom in the suite, and while she was gone, Jack poured fresh drinks for both of them and took his over to the long beige sectional in the living area. The square coffee table in front of the couch was glass, too.

Jack set his glass down, anyway.

And thought of Erica.

Every time she laughed, every time she moved, every time she spoke, every time those dark-brown eyes met his, every time he remembered that he was going to tell her goodbye and never see her again, Jack felt as if he'd been punched. He'd never wanted a woman as badly as he wanted Erica Cooley.

And yet, when he considered chucking it all, giving up the crusade to save others where he hadn't been able to save his own, he knew he couldn't do it. When he thought about changing his life, his goals, his mind filled with visions of that tiny body, that small casket and he realized he couldn't turn his back on all the lives he *could* save.

He couldn't risk committing himself that completely again, either.

He laid his head back, eyes closed, waiting for her. Trying to predict whether she'd join him on the couch. Or make the smart choice and stay over at the table.

He tried to figure out what he hoped she'd do.

She joined him on the couch—a full cushion away. He still hadn't decided if he wanted her there, or across the room where he wouldn't have to be so strong.

He'd had a lot to drink.

Jack leaned forward, grabbed his glass from the table and took a full sip. He didn't look at her.

"What are you thinking about?" The soft words touched him, seemed so intimate.

"When Melissa and Courtney were killed, something inside me changed. Shut down."

It still felt odd, talking about that part of his life. He never had before tonight. And yet, strangely, it felt right. The environment was safe, somehow.

He wanted Erica to know.

His arm lay along the back of the couch and she reached out with her hand, laying it on his.

"How could it not?" she asked gently. "They were a big part of you."

"Far more than I'd realized," he admitted. "If I'd allowed myself to acknowledge how important they were to me, I'd never have been able to do the job I'd chosen, risking my life every day."

"You didn't work in an FBI office?"

He shook his head, remembering some of the more dangerous situations he'd somehow managed to get through unscathed. "I was a field agent. Drug trafficking." He'd slammed into more than one hovel filled with greasy, violent, conscienceless men, who'd pull their guns without the least provocation.

"I didn't train for the crisis team until after Melissa's death."

Her fingers trailed lightly over the back of his hand. "Whenever you've talked about the past few years, you've mentioned your work, things you do in your spare time, skiing, books you've read, movies, trips to Vegas. What about your personal life?''

"That *is* my personal life. Work and what I do in my spare time. I'm out of town a lot, but I have an apartment here in New York.''

Erica looked down shyly, which was not like her. "I mean your *really* personal life," she said. "You haven't said so, but there must be a woman in the city someplace who's missed having your company this week. Someone who would've had it if I, if we—''

"There's no one." He wasn't sure how smart it was to tell her that. But he wasn't sure about a lot of things at the moment.

Except that he hadn't had enough whiskey to dull his senses. He took another sip.

"How long has it been since there's been someone?" If he'd detected jealousy in her voice, he might've been able to joke with her, fob off the question—while secretly being flattered, of course.

He couldn't build any defenses against Erica's compassion.

"I told you, I don't have the time or energy to invest in 'someone.' Nor can I do my job if I know someone's waiting at home for me. How can I take the chance of putting them through the hell and the horror I went through when Melissa and Courtney were killed? I risk my life every single time I go to work. As a freelance negotiator there's very little I do that's safe. I don't man a desk during downtimes or give training classes, do research or program management like I used to do with the agency.''

"But you must have friends.''

"Of course I do.'' He had acquaintances all over the United States. Guys he could call if he ever needed a favor. Usually he just called them to go out for a beer if he was in town.

Or to bum a place to crash for a few nights.

Jack hated hotels.

"And you must have sex.''

It took Jack a second to recover from the jolt those words sent through his body.

"I mean, you're a gorgeous man, Jack. You exude virility, energy. Vitality. Sex appeal...''

"I have sex,'' Jack choked out, a bit desperate to shut her up. "Sometimes. Not often. And not with anyone exclusively.''

"Oh. Good.''

He finished off his whiskey, set the glass on the table, much harder than he'd intended. He winced at the sound.

"You know the part of me that shut down after Melissa?''

He felt foreign to himself, talking this way, but he couldn't let tonight end without telling her.

"Yeah.''

"I discovered this week that it wasn't permanent.''

Her fingers froze on his wrist.

"It's okay,'' he assured her quickly, wondering if perhaps the whiskey was affecting him, after all.

"You aren't supposed to *do* anything with that knowledge. I'm not *asking* for anything, I just wanted you to know. Wanted to thank you."

He couldn't tell what she was thinking. She wouldn't meet his eyes.

And...damn, her lips were trembling.

"Ah, Erica," he said, trying to cajole her into calmness. Into repose and resignation. Instead, he was afraid he'd only let her hear his own despondency.

She smiled, but it looked like an effort.

He felt utterly useless. His muscles tensed with the effort it was taking him just to sit there.

Her shoulders straightened. She looked at him, her eyes glistening.

And all his strength dissolved.

CHAPTER THREE

THERE WAS NOTHING sexual about the way he pulled her into his arms. Jack wasn't sure what was right and what was wrong anymore; he knew only that he couldn't sit there with Erica hurting so badly and do nothing.

Which was why she ended up cradled in his arms, her face pressed against his chest as she took a couple of ragged breaths.

"I'm sorry," she whispered.

"Don't be," he said softly, aching for both of them. "Please don't ever be sorry we met."

Her eyes shone with tears that didn't fall. "I'm not sorry we met," she said, her voice weak. "I *am* sorry I'm not better equipped to handle this."

"How could you be?" He sat back, pulling her with him, allowing her to rest against him more than actually holding her. "I don't think either of us was prepared for what's happened."

"I never expected to fall for someone."

"Me, neither, which is why we couldn't possibly have been prepared."

They were quiet for a while, the hum of the hotel's air conditioner, her weight against him, lulling Jack

into a tentative sense of peace. He started to follow
Erica's breathing pattern, soothed by the evenness,
the steady ebb and flow. He wondered if she'd fallen
asleep.

Part of him hoped so.

Another part, the possessive part that he'd thought
gone from him forever, didn't want to waste a single
second of the time still left to them. There were so
many thoughts—so many feelings—inside her and
he wanted every one of them. To store them away,
like tiny gifts, to pull out and savor in the years to
come.

"I'm not sorry about us."

She wasn't asleep.

"I'm not, either," Jack said.

As frustrated and horrible as he felt, he *should*
wish he'd never met her. Shouldn't he?

"Can I ask you something?" he said a moment
later.

"Sure." She was playing with the corner of his
collar, rubbing it back and forth against the pad of
her thumb.

"Sex with Jefferson—he's good to you, isn't he?"

It wasn't any of his damn business. And yet it was.
He loved her. He needed to know that she was
treated right.

He needed to know.

"Jefferson is always good to me."

Jack had suspected as much. And was genuinely
comforted to hear her say it.

He was also far more jealous than he had any right to be.

"I just wasn't sure, with him being so much older..." *Let it go, man.*

"Sex doesn't really play a big part in our relationship." The words were said quietly but not hesitantly. Jack sat unmoving, wanting to hear more, wanting her more. He shifted beneath her to hide—and perhaps ease—the tightness in his groin.

"When we were first married we tried...Jefferson was a very conscientious lover, always making sure I was...satisfied before he...you know."

So the man wasn't a selfish bastard, but then, after a week of hearing about him, Jack already knew that.

"After a while, I don't know, things just tapered off. We rarely make love anymore."

"Did you ever discuss it? Ask him about it?"

"We talked." Her knuckle grazed his throat.

"And?"

"One reason's his age. The male sex drive dropping after fifty and all that. But Jefferson is very fit. He doesn't look or act anywhere near the fifty-nine he actually is."

"So what was the other reason?"

She turned her head, burying her face in his chest for a moment. Jack held his breath, willing his body not to torment him.

Finally she said, "He knows my heart isn't in it."

Jack didn't know what to say to that. He was ashamed of his immediate reaction—the fact that he felt glad Jefferson wasn't having sex very often with the woman he'd fallen so suddenly in love with. He was also saddened to think of Erica going through the rest of her life practically untouched.

"I told you I was an only child," she said, her body growing heavier against his as she relaxed. "What I didn't say was that my parents were already in their forties when I was conceived. My dad was seventy when he died six years ago. Jefferson's fifteen years younger than him, but somehow he'd seemed like a second father to me."

"What about your mother? Is she still alive?"

Jack's parents were both gone—killed in a car accident when he was in college.

"She's in Florida," Erica said. "Living in an adult community next door to her younger sister. They golf and play bridge all day."

"What did she think of your marriage?"

"She was mostly for it," Erica said. "She wasn't thrilled about the age difference, but she knew I'd never find a man better than Jeff...."

Her voice trailed off again and Jack tried not to think as he held her. Until she shuddered.

"Erica?"

She raised her head and he could see the agony in her eyes.

"This is just so hard," she said, her lips twisted in pain. "I never expected it to be so hard."

"I know...."

"What are we going to do?"

"What *can* we do?"

As she watched him silently, Jack's heart took hope. He waited to see what miracle she might come up with, some way they could be true to themselves and yet...

"Nothing," she said. "Keeping in touch would not only be incredibly stupid, it would make things even harder. I'll survive in my real world, if you're no more than just a memory. You have to be something I can put away when I go home. If you were still a part of my life, I'd constantly be wanting more."

He knew she was right, but...

"Maybe you should at least have my address, just in case."

"No, Jack. I'm not strong enough to do that. I'd be tired one night, feeling lonely, and I'd end up using it."

"In my line of work, you don't want to be too easily found, so I'm not listed."

"Good."

He nodded. This was the way it had to be.

"Oh, God, why does life have to be so hard?" She sounded beaten.

Her face was only inches from his, and Jack leaned forward slightly to kiss her eyelids closed. She should get some rest. She had a meeting in the morning. He could sit there and hold her the rest of the night.

Hold her and not think.

His lips trailed tenderly across one cheek and then the other and then had nowhere else to go.

Except down to her mouth.

There was no conscious decision. No decision at all. The hour was late, the alcohol convincing. The need to comfort, to connect, too overpowering.

One minute he was kissing her face…and the next she was naked beneath him and his lips were on her breast, her nipple, his body sliding inside hers.

It was wrong. He knew that. And he could see, by the look in her eyes, that she knew it, too.

And yet, nothing had ever felt more right.

They had two hours before she had to shower and leave. Jack made love to her, laughed with her, told her how beautiful she was, how smart, how much he admired her.

And then, in the doorway of her hotel room, just before dawn, he told her goodbye.

A COUPLE OF MONTHS later, in the bedroom she shared with Jefferson, Erica knew for certain that she'd never be able to forget Jack.

Or forgive herself for that stolen week in New York.

She and Jefferson had just returned from a pre-holiday party at the White House. He was still in his tux, although he'd loosened the tie at his neck. He was sitting on the love seat in the corner of the big bedroom suite in their Washington condo. He looked tired.

"When are you going to tell me what's the matter?" he asked as she came in from the bathroom.

Now. She had to tell him now. But...

"Why do you say that?" She wanted to take off the long, slim-fitting black gown and pull on her silk pajamas. But she didn't.

"I've known something was wrong ever since you came home from New York," he said, running his hands through his thick, stylishly cut gray hair.

"Why didn't you mention it before?"

"I'd hoped that eventually you'd come to me with whatever it was."

Were his shoulders as broad as Jack's?

Surprisingly enough, Erica thought, they probably were.

But were they broad enough to handle what she was about to tell him? She'd been cold all evening, the November chill seeping through her bones. But now she was sweating.

Wanting nothing more than to crawl into the big four-poster bed, cuddle up to her husband and go to sleep, Erica joined Jefferson on the other side of the room, where she dropped into an armchair adjacent to the love seat. She didn't know where to begin. Or how.

Jefferson waited. And Erica knew how much it was costing him to do this. Her husband always anticipated crises, always acted decisively, attempting to resolve problems if he couldn't prevent them. Asking him to just sit and do nothing wasn't fair.

"I never realized it was possible to hate myself so much," she said in a low voice.

He leaned forward, elbows on his knees. "Knowing you as I do, I'm sure there's no need to put yourself through that kind of grief, Erica, so why don't we talk about whatever this is and get it behind us?"

If he had any idea...

Erica opened her mouth to speak but, looking up at him, couldn't make the words come. How could she do this to him? She, who knew so well how devastating it was to be betrayed?

After suffering the effects of Shane's betrayal, she'd never have believed herself capable of doing anything so deplorable. So selfish. So hideously unfair.

Her stomach roiled, and Erica was afraid she might be sick again.

"I met a man in New York."

Jefferson's head dropped.

"His name's Jack Shaw. He's a hostage negotiator, used to be with the FBI."

Her husband's shoulders straightened as he sat back and held his head up to meet her gaze.

"You want a divorce. To go to him."

"I'm never going to see him again."

She had no way of seeing him, even if she wanted to, which she didn't. Her life and Jack's—they were farther apart than ever.

Jefferson's eyes narrowed. "He left you?" If Erica hadn't been feeling so completely miserable, she'd have smiled at the delivery of that question. His tone said *How dare he leave you?* as though Jefferson himself was ready to go hunt the man down.

She shook her head, instead.

"We both knew when we left New York that we'd never see each other again."

"Why not?"

She did smile then, though tremulously. "I'm a married woman, Jefferson."

"That's more in name than in deed," he said sadly. "And I was aware from the outset this might happen. Hell, Erica, I'm old enough to be your father. You think I haven't been prepared for this from the beginning?"

"No," she said, a little shocked.

"Well, I was." His posture was relaxed; only the fact that he couldn't seem to figure out what to do with his hands revealed his inner turmoil. "I'm not going to stand in your way. And I sure as hell don't want you feeling beholden to me."

Erica felt as though her world was spinning increasingly out of control.

She wanted to tell him she'd married him for better or worse. That she'd never—once—had any intention of forsaking those vows or asking to be released from them.

But she *had* forsaken them.

In the worst possible way.

It all came pouring out then. How Jack had saved her from that jerk at Maggie's. How they'd never planned to see each other again, but how they'd each shown up at Maggie's the next night, just in case the other might happen to stop by. How they did the same thing every night that week. How they talked. And never touched. Never even went anywhere else.

How she'd have come home in a second if she could have gotten the *Journal* reporter to talk to her.

Jefferson nodded at that point.

She told him about Jack's wife and daughter. His job. How he, no less than Erica, wasn't free to embark on a relationship.

"We accepted from the beginning that one week was all we were ever going to have."

Reaching across the space between them, Jefferson pulled her from the chair and into his arms, his touch comforting, completely nonsexual. "We've nursed you through a broken heart before, my dear," he said, sounding certain, if a little tired. "We can do so again."

She wished a broken heart was the only consequence of her time with Jack. "I don't deserve you," she whispered, fighting tears.

"Don't talk like that," he said, his voice soothing. "You can't be blamed for being attracted to a man your own age. It's natural."

"You have to be disappointed in me."

"I am disappointed," he admitted with a heavy sigh, and the knife inside Erica twisted further. "But not in you."

"How could you not be?"

"Because I know you, Erica, and I know that you'd never purposely do this—to either of us. How can I blame you for being human?"

"You're far too generous."

"Marrying you was the most reckless thing I've ever done," he said, gazing into her eyes. "I'm almost three decades older than you. I know, and I've always known, that our marriage contravenes the natural order of things. As I said, I don't fault you for what you did. What you felt..."

"But you're disappointed, anyway."

"I'm disappointed that I'm not twenty years younger, that when I finally fell head over heels in love with a woman, she wasn't my own age and at the same place in life. I'm disappointed that I'm too old to do for you whatever this Jack guy did."

Erica started to feel sick again. She freed herself from her husband's arms, whispering, "There's more."

"You slept with him."

Though it took more strength than she thought she had, Erica forced herself to keep looking at him. "How did you know?"

"I suspected as much the day you got back. Don't forget, honey, I've taken you there myself. You get a certain look about you after you've made love. A softness, a satisfied peace. It's a look I haven't seen in a long time."

Only someone as attuned to her as Jefferson would notice such a thing.

"I'm so sorry, Jeff," she said hoarsely. "I can't believe I've done this. That I've hurt you like this. I didn't think I could do such a thing. And certainly never wanted to."

"I know," he said, his eyes filled with the sadness he wouldn't express in words.

"I'd do anything to take it all back...."

"I know that, too," he said, and then held her hand, much like she'd held Jack's that night he'd told her about losing his wife and daughter. "Of course, it would've been best if you'd walked away before there was anything to take back, but if I think that way, I'm going to get angry and that won't do us any good."

"You *should* be angry."

He bowed his head, and she couldn't see what he was thinking. "No," he finally said, looking up at her. "Anger is unproductive and so is regret. Rather than wishing for the impossible, the wiser thing to do would be for us to put this behind us and move forward."

Did he want a divorce?

"Forward how?"

"If, as you say, there's no chance of a relationship between you and this man, if you still want to continue living the life we've created here, I see no reason for anything to change. Our reasons for marrying still stand. I still love you, want to take care of you. Professionally, I still need a wife...."

She didn't say anything. Couldn't.

Because there was more. Something that prevented her from ever returning to Jack.

But something she didn't think Jefferson should have to accept, either.

CHAPTER FOUR

SHE HAD SOMETHING else to tell him.

Senator Jefferson Cooley sat next to his beautiful young wife on the pale beige seat and waited.

He could handle whatever she had to say. She wasn't leaving him. That was all that mattered—Erica allowing him to share her life.

He was one hell of a lucky man.

Or a pathetic man?

Where that thought came from, he didn't know. But as his wife looked at him, her eyes brimming with unshed tears, with soul-deep sorrow, with panic and a despair that went beyond anything he'd ever read there before, the thought just disappeared.

"What is it, love?" he asked, holding both her hands in his. Whatever it took, he'd make it right for her.

"I...I'm..."

His heart grew cold.

"I'm pregnant."

Oh.

Hell.

He stared at her. Acid burning his stomach. His chest. Every living part of him.

He preferred the cold.

"I'm sorry, Jeff. So sorry." Erica didn't cry often, which made the tears sliding down her beautiful cheeks that much more threatening. He wondered if tears were falling down his, as well.

Or if the pain was too deep for that.

"It's okay," he said. Because *he* wanted it to be.

Out of the blue he thought of her father. A high-powered attorney, Jefferson's friend. Would he have approved of Jefferson's marriage to his daughter? Or would he be finding this night just reward for Jefferson's sin, his transgression in marrying a woman so much younger?

"No." She shook her head, pulling one hand free to run soft fingertips along the side of his face.

Wiping away tears?

"It's not okay." Her sweet voice tore at him. Making him want to destroy something—preferably the man who could do for her what he could not.

It touched that chord of love deep inside him, as well.

She was so strong. But she was lost, too. He could see the confusion, the fear and need in her dark-brown eyes as she gazed at him. And it occurred to him that she was there with *him*. In their bedroom.

He was the one she came to when she had a problem. The one who heard her confessions. Who shared the realities of everyday life with her.

"We'll make it okay," he told her. "We always do."

"You shouldn't have to," she said, and there was no doubt that she meant the words she was saying. "I can't do this to you, Jeff. And yet, I guess I already have. It's not as though I can just disappear out of your life. The press would be all over you—us—in a second."

A surge of hurt, disguised as anger, shot through him. Even now, did it always have to be about work?

Couldn't it ever be just about the two of them? The team they made? Their ability to face anything life had to offer as long as they did it together?

"Leave the press out of this."

"We can't."

The anguish cut a little more deeply. "The press is a surface concern, Erica. There are no reporters here in our home. In our bedroom." *In our life. The life I share with you, the life no one else knows about.*

She didn't say anything. Just continued to gaze at him with those sorrowful eyes.

"Right now it's just you and me, love."

She looked down.

So did he.

At the flat stomach he'd been admiring in that alarmingly gorgeous gown she'd been wearing so elegantly all evening.

You, me and another man's baby, he amended. So heartsick he was dizzy for a moment.

Even if it hadn't been months since he'd made love to his wife, the baby she was carrying couldn't be his. During his early twenties, Jefferson had contracted mumps. He'd been left sterile.

"What do you want to do?" He found the question floating somewhere in the red haze of his mind.

"I have no idea." She shook her head, looked up at him with complete honesty. "I know it's ludicrous and completely unfair, but all I've been able to think about is talking to you. It's what I always do when I can't figure something out."

A patch of clearness appeared in the haze. "So let's start with the basics," he said.

She needed him to help her sort out the problem. He knew how to do that.

She needed him. He could think again.

"I'm pregnant," she said, as though making a list. "I'm never seeing Jack again."

"You're going to have the baby." He knew that wasn't an option. He was, publicly at least, a right-to-lifer. She was, too.

Before life had become so confused, he'd been a right-to-lifer, period. But he'd been in Washington a long time. He'd heard stories, seen things. Too many things. He wasn't sure where he stood, personally, on most issues anymore. There were always two sides.

With good people, well-intentioned people, on each of them.

Erica was staring at him, her eyes wide. Startled. He raised his brows in question.

"I hadn't thought that far ahead," she said, sounding more like the little girl of twelve she'd been when he'd first met her twenty years before.

Since he'd married Erica, people had been saying he'd robbed the cradle. No one knew that, most of the time, Erica was the more mature of the two. She was so determined. So focused and sure of her course.

She sat tall, holding herself rigid, one slim body against the world—hiding so much. He'd never seen Erica let herself need anyone. *Except for me,* he reminded himself. That stood for something. Everything.

Jefferson's needs vanished. His fears, the pain and disappointment, were buried beneath the compulsion that was stronger than self.

Picking Erica up, he cradled her like a child. Carried her to their bed. Lay down with her, turning her so he could spoon his body around hers. Enveloping her in his safety. He did this because she allowed herself to take comfort from him.

For those moments Jefferson did what he could to protect her from the agonies of living.

Just as he'd been trying to do—in one way or another—for most of her life. Far more important than career, fantasies or ambitions, Erica was everything to him. Precious. It didn't matter that she couldn't return his love, that she couldn't love him the same way he loved her.

Eventually Erica turned over, cuddled next to him, her pale face only an inch from his own. "I don't know how to protect you from this," she said. "I can't stand it that you're going to be irrevocably hurt, no matter what. That you've done nothing, and yet you'll pay the greatest price."

Done nothing? He'd married a woman young enough to be his daughter. Robbed her of the chance to find a man who could raise the passion of youth in her.

A man who could give her children.

But for now, none of that was important. Now they were solving problems. Dealing with facts.

"Don't you think you should contact your Jack?" *Her* Jack. He hated those words, punished himself with them.

"I can't."

"Why not?" Tense, Jeff waited to hear that the other man had used Erica and then dumped her. Waited, knowing he'd have to fight the urge to hunt the other man down and kill him with his bare hands.

"Because I don't have any way to find him."

"He refused to give you even that much?" The acid was back.

"No, he tried. I didn't *want* to know how to find him."

"Because of me."

"Yes."

He'd spent the past three years reaching for heaven. And landed in hell.

"So we'll track him down."

"No, Jeff. In the first place, he's unlisted."

"He's FBI."

"Ex. He's independent. And good. You know as well as I do that means he'll be untraceable. They'll protect him. He doesn't exist."

Still, there were ways. "And in the second place?"

"It won't make any difference to him."

"Trust me," he told her, lying as close to her as he could get. "It'll make a difference."

When she shook her head, dark tendrils of that short textured hairstyle he loved flew around her eyes. Making her look wild. Making him feel a little wild.

She was his wife, dammit.

His.

"The baby will only be more reason to stay away from me," she said softly.

Jeff was finding it hard to believe that Erica had fallen for such an insensitive son of a bitch.

"It's too late for him, Jeff."

He listened while Erica gave him the horrifying account of two deaths—Jack Shaw's wife and his baby daughter. Listened to her words, but heard how much Erica loved the other man. Heard the way her voice softened and knew that he was never going to instill that kind of love in her.

Heard and felt hope die.

And yet he knew she was probably right: It *was* too late for Jack.

"And even if there wasn't all that to contend

with," she said, her mouth still only an inch from his, "there's his job. There's no way a man like Jack could risk his life every day if he knew he was leaving behind someone who needed him every bit as much as the person he was going to save—because when he goes to work there's the possibility that he'll have to offer his life in exchange for that of a hostage.

"The only way he can cope with Melissa and Courtney's deaths is by spending his time preventing the same thing from happening to someone else. It makes their lives—and their deaths—count. They didn't die in vain."

Jefferson could understand that, too.

"So who has to know the baby isn't mine? Other than you, I haven't told anyone I'm sterile in over thirty years." Jeff's heart started to pound. Was he really considering fatherhood at his age?

Adrenaline pumped through him. He felt a new surge of life, excitement and anticipation.

Him. A father. It was a dream he'd given up forty years ago.

Erica sat up. Her gown had slipped, revealing more of her cleavage than she normally exposed. "I can't let you do that, Jeff," she said. "I love you too much to see you make such a sacrifice."

She loved him.

The front of his tuxedo pants was fuller than when he'd zipped them up a few hours ago.

"What sacrifice?" he asked, thinking quickly.

Desperately. He had a chance to keep the woman he loved.

He looked up at her. Her flawless skin, full lips. The honesty blazing from her beautiful eyes.

There was still a chance.

"All I've ever wanted was to be able to share your life with you," he reminded her. "To be the one you came home to each night. To hear about your day, share in your triumphs. Be there to support you through the tough times. Hear you laugh. See the world through your eyes. So having the opportunity to be the father of your child—" he had to think of it as hers, only hers "—to share that rewarding experience with you is a bonus."

Tears sprang to her eyes again. "Only you could put a positive spin on this," she said, her lips breaking into a tremulous smile.

"The solution works," he said, making sure his point hit home. "I get what I want—you. The baby gets what it deserves—a set of parents who will love and provide for it. You get the security and love you've always had here. Help with your baby. Friendship..."

With one hand, the nails perfectly manicured, Erica traced his lips. "You don't have to sell me on what I get," she said softly. "I've always known what a treasure I have in you. You're the one who deserves so much more...."

Maybe. Sometimes he thought so. But he loved *her*.

"So, we're having a baby?" he asked, making sure they'd sealed their bargain.

Erica, with marked hesitation, nodded. "On the condition that if you change your mind, you promise to let me know. I won't have you tied down to this unless it's what you truly want."

He had no doubt about what he wanted.

And suddenly, no choice but to take it. Reaching up, sliding one hand around her neck, he pulled her lips to his, taking them in a kiss that was far more demanding than any he'd taken before. He filled her with his own taste, as though he could somehow wipe away the other man. Not only from her senses, but from her memory.

That night, Jefferson set out to seduce his wife. To have her even if she didn't love him.

That night, the man who always put her welfare first was tired. He was a man who needed her, and Erica let him find his comfort in her body.

There are many kinds of love. That was his last coherent thought before he drifted off to sleep.

CHAPTER FIVE

May 1997

JACK SHAW belonged to his job.

For better or worse.

Patience was his virtue. Staying cool under pressure his MO.

A woman—the mother—was crying. Getting hysterical. Jack refused to let himself hear her. She wanted him to do something.

She didn't understand that timing was the key to survival. To her daughter's survival.

He understood her, though. He knew exactly how she was feeling as she waited there in the balmy May sunshine. Helpless while her daughter's life was held in the precarious hands of a maniac.

Marissa was only four, he'd been told. She was on campus as part of a child-care program.

Rubber-suited men in bullet-proof vests and gas masks surrounded the building. A team was working on the classroom ceiling; tubes with tiny lenses were being fed down through the air-conditioning vents so they could see inside the classroom on the television monitor set up in the van.

"Do you like dogs, James?" Jack asked. He'd been sitting on the cement outside a first-floor classroom window for half an hour. This was one tough talk-down.

"What's it matter?" came the surly reply through the barely open window.

"I had a dog when I was kid. Damnedest thing, though. He was my best friend, and the biggest pain in my ass, too. Barking and getting me in trouble when I would've been able to sneak in past curfew undetected. Waking me up early to be put out on Saturday mornings, the only time I could sleep late."

There was no sound from the classroom. Jack wanted to hear something—anything—from Marissa. Even crying.

He listened. But heard nothing. And so he sat, pretending he had all the time in the world.

Another high school. Arizona this time. Jack had been in Los Angeles visiting an old buddy from his time with the agency—and attending a movie premiere as the guest of a director he'd once rescued. Arizona authorities had been relieved he was so close.

Sometime over the years Jack's specialty had become child negotiation.

"So," he said again, dropping a couple of small stones from one hand to the other. "You like dogs?" The list on the ground beside him—the one he'd memorized but kept referring to, anyway—said that James had always wanted a dog.

There was no answer from inside.

The compilation of facts about the teenager had

been written by James's teachers, but his mother had been one of the main contributors. She knew her son well. Too bad she hadn't done anything with that knowledge. Like to understand what drove him, what made him so unhappy—so desperate. Try to help him.

These were the cases that sickened Jack the most. The parents who were so shocked to find their son or daughter capable of terrorism. Parents who only knew their kids in superficial ways, who didn't recognize the misery or the rage.

"James? You like dogs?"

"Maybe." The tone was belligerent, but Jack smiled, anyway. James had just come down a step.

"So, you know why the poor dog chased its tail?" Nothing.

"He was trying to make ends meet."

The ground was hard beneath his butt, but Jack pretended not to notice. He was just there for a chat. For as long as it took.

"You ready to tell me what you want?" he asked in a casual voice.

"A dog. Can you get me a dog?"

"I'll work on it." Jack waited. "That's all you want?" he asked, leaning back against the stucco wall of the building.

The fifteen-year-old didn't answer.

"You ready to come out, then?" he called easily. "Or to send Marissa out, at least?"

"We got a picture!" The exclamation was a whisper—from the bearded, longhaired police officer working closest to Jack. He rolled a television monitor into Jack's line of vision.

The boy with the deep sullen voice wasn't even five feet tall. He was skinnier than a girl. He wore clean, stylishly baggy slacks and a pullover. His blond hair was cut short. James Talmadge looked like every mother's dream.

Sweat dripped down the back of Jack's neck.

The dream ended where James's right hand held a gun to a four-year-old girl's throat. Marissa was lying on the floor, shaking, her eyes wide, unfocused.

Goddammit!

What was it with high schools and guns, anyway? High-school terrorism had happened enough times you'd think someone would do something about teenage anger before it got to this point.

Jack suddenly heard a painful wail. The little girl's mother had just seen the television. On the monitor the child jerked, probably recognizing her mother's voice.

"Get her out of here," Jack said, pointing to the mother as, on the screen, James pushed the end of his handgun against the child's throat.

Marissa's mother wasn't leaving without a fight. A female officer spoke to her, telling her that for Marissa's sake she had to at least move back and be quiet. Hearing her mother's voice, knowing that her mother was right outside the window, could make the child do something rash that would get her killed.

Jack saw the young mother nod, her shoulders racked with sobs as she allowed herself to be led several feet away.

The mother's anguish singed his nerve endings. It had been a long time since he'd felt that particular blistering. Usually he managed to distance himself from the pain of others. It was the only way he could do his job.

"James, we're working on the dog," he said, maintaining his patience. He stared at the laces of his tennis shoes and the hem of his jeans, which rode half an inch up his ankle. "You can trust me. Just toss me the gun and it'll all be over. You'll be safe," he finished calmly, as though he were encouraging the boy to throw a baseball.

There was no answer.

"You know what happened when the dog went to the flea market?" he asked, his nonchalant tone belying the intensity with which he studied the screen. "He stole the show."

Timing was the key to survival. The longer he could stall the harried boy, the more chance he had of talking him down. Or at least getting little Marissa out of there.

Though he could see the two kids, he still listened attentively. The little girl's unnatural quiet bothered him. The resiliency and adaptability of children was amazing, but Marissa's mind was going to catch up with her eventually.

Maybe today. Maybe ten years from now.

And it was going to be hell for her when it did.

"Tell me what you want, James."

"You got that dog?"

"Like I said, I'm working on it." Turning to the officer on his right, Jack whispered, "Get me a dog."

Nodding, the young man took off at a trot.

"What else?" he asked. A dog was not the reason the kid had barged into a classroom brandishing a gun. Jack would bet his life it wasn't the reason he'd cleared out everyone but the four-year-old child he now held hostage.

"I want my little sister back," James said. He still had the gun on the child, but he'd turned toward the window. Looking for Jack?

"Where is she?"

"In a foster home."

Jack scanned the paper he'd been given. There was nothing about a broken family there. With raised brows, he glanced around at the officers surrounding him. They shrugged, shook their heads. The school principal was there. When Jack met his eye, he nodded.

Shit. It was information he should've had an hour ago.

"So, Mr. Hotshot Cop, you gonna make the trade? You gonna bring me my sister?"

Chances were he couldn't. But Jack wasn't going to tell the kid no. Number-one rule of engagement— never tell the perpetrator no. The word signified endings.

"I'll see what I can do," he said, instead.

"Yeah, you do that."

Marissa was crying. Jack couldn't hear her, but he saw a tear drip off her chin.

James saw it, too. The boy stared at the teardrop for a long moment. And bent down to wipe the little girl's cheeks.

She glanced up at her captor, terror on her face, before her expression once again went blank.

Jack took a deep breath. Calmed the shudders rushing through him. "Hey, James, you ready to come out?" he asked. "We'll do everything we can to get your sister back, I promise."

"Yeah, right." There was no mistaking the boy's bitterness. "I've heard that before. I've waited almost a year."

"But I'm here now," Jack said. "And I promise I won't leave until I've gotten to the bottom of this."

"Don't screw with me, man," the boy said. "I know how it works. As soon as you get this kid, they put handcuffs on me and *adios.*. You're gone, never to be heard from again. And Brittney's left with some guy who slaps her for wanting more than one glass of milk at dinner."

Lowering his head, Jack felt the ache of years' worth of struggle climbing up the back of his neck. An officer handed him a couple of typed paragraphs on a computer printout. Information he should've had an hour ago, except that the boy's mother hadn't thought it was pertinent.

James's mother had never been married. Had had several live-in boyfriends, but only two children, James and Brittney. By two different fathers. Neither father was in the picture. Ms. Talmadge had lost custody of her three-year-old daughter because of repeated abuse. And since Child Protective Services was attempting to place Brittney in a permanent home with a new family, James had been denied visitation rights.

"How do you know her foster father slaps her?"

"She told me."

"You've seen her?"

"Yeah."

"Where?"

"I go by her day care sometimes. Talk to her through the fence. Now, I mean it, man, get me Brittney—and a dog—and I'll make the trade." He jabbed the gun at Marissa's throat.

"You know why the dog didn't speak to his hind foot?"

James turned toward the window. "What's with the jokes, man?"

"The dog didn't speak to his foot because it's not polite to talk back to your paw."

The skinny teenager shook his head, but his shoulders visibly relaxed.

Jack checked the list. He asked James a couple of questions about various friends named there. About the volleyball team he played on. James's only response was to adjust the gun at Marissa's throat. His hand was shaking.

"You know why dogs wag their tails?"

James looked at the window.

"Because no one else will do it for them."

The kid gave a disgusted snort. He was still looking in the direction of Jack's voice.

"You know how to tell if you have a stupid dog?"

Carefully monitoring the activity around him, waiting for the appearance of the dog, Jack continued sitting on the ground as though nothing was going on.

"It chases parked cars," he said.

The little girl was lying still, her cheek pressed to the tile of the classroom floor. Her eyes were open, unmoving, staring vacantly at the floor.

"James, tell me again how you think holding Marissa is going to help you get Brittney?"

"Because it's an even trade. A little girl for a little girl," he spat.

Although this emotionally disturbed kid's thinking was clearly twisted, there was no doubting his confidence in this theory he'd worked out.

The entire team of uniformed men and women were watching Jack. And the monitor. They were standing by in case Jack ran out of time. Waiting for a signal from him to move in.

James leaned back against a desk. It slid, toppled, caught the boy on the ankle.

From the open window Jack heard the crash. An angrily whispered *Shit.*

"James? You okay in there?"

"Like you care."

"Believe it or not, I do care." And he did. In an objective sense, as an observer. It was what made him so good at his job. He had to care. Because if he didn't, he'd never be able to reach his perpetrators.

If he didn't find a way to empathize, he'd lose his sanity by hating.

Hating every single person like James who put innocent people in danger.

Hating the young man who'd aimed his gun at Melissa's chest and—

No! He knew better than that. He had a job to do.

For the poor distraught woman who stood only a few yards away from him trembling in the arms of a young blond man in business attire. Slacks. A tie. White shirt. His expression was a mixture of fear and unadulterated rage. He must be the father.

The two were counting on Jack to remain calm.

He asked James about the high-school football season. About getting his driver's license. And what kind of plans he had for a car.

The boy didn't respond.

Marissa was starting to shake. Her entire body was shivering, as though she was lying in a snowdrift rather than on a schoolroom floor.

Around the corner of the van Jack became aware of movement. A uniformed police officer approached him, a beagle puppy in her arms.

"We got the dog, James," Jack said even before he had possession of the animal. The officer was approaching from the side of the building, staying out of the boy's sight—and shot.

"He's a puppy," Jack said as the woman leaned over to hand him the squirming five-pound ball of brown, white and black fur. "He's got big brown eyes and he's all yours."

Holding his breath, Jack studied the monitor. Obviously more agitated, James stared at the little girl.

"You want me to bring him in?" Jack asked.

"What I want is my sister." The boy's words, delivered through gritted teeth, were fierce. "You got her out there, Cop?"

"We're working on it."

"Yeah, well, work a little faster. I'm not waitin' around here much longer."

Marissa, who'd started to cry openly, received an angry kick. "Shut up!"

Through the open window, Jack heard the growled command. James moved and Jack stiffened, his hand at his belt, ready to pull his gun.

Reaching up, gaze on the monitor, he dropped the puppy through the window. And ignored the new sheen of sweat that broke out on his upper lip when James barely glanced at the dog.

"Get up," the kid told the little girl. She didn't move.

"I said get up!" James ordered.

Marissa's body convulsed, and then she settled back, a quivering mass. With the gun never moving from her throat, James one-handedly pulled the child's arms behind her, yanked off his belt and strapped Marissa's hands together. The little girl didn't even try to fight him. He dragged her over to a far corner, to the left of where Jack was sitting.

"Don't move."

Keeping the gun pointed at the child, James moved to the puppy and pushed it back through the window. Jack caught the small shaking dog and handed it to the nearest officer.

"Get my sister here in the next five minutes or I shoot," James yelled just above Jack's head. Close enough to slide his hand out that window and shoot Jack.

"We're working on it, James," Jack said, as though reassuring a hungry boy that dinner was almost ready. "But it might take a little longer than five minutes."

The gun still aimed in the general direction of the little girl, the boy fired a shot. Splinters from the chalkboard sprayed around the room. The bullet lodged in the cement wall.

Uniform and rubber-suited officers alike jerked to attention. All eyes were on Jack, guns pointing toward the classroom.

"I have a shot," one of the officers said. "Should I take it?"

"No."

Jack wasn't going to see that boy die if he could help it.

He'd have to go in. James was shooting. It was only a matter of time.

Marissa was lying to the left of the window. James was on the right. Jack's job was to get through that window and put himself between the child and the gun.

The worst that could happen was that he'd take the bullet. He hoped it would hit the bullet-proof vest he had on under his T-shirt. But if not, it would be his life in exchange for the child's.

Small price to pay.

He shifted onto his knees. "James?" he called. "My butt's getting sore sitting here, so I'm going to stand and lean on the windowsill. Okay?"

It was a gamble. But if the boy's attention was on Jack, chances were the child would be safe for another moment or two.

"I don't want you to be startled by the movement," he said, crouching under the window. "Is it okay with you if I look in?" he asked.

"No."

Peering over his shoulder, receiving the confirmation he'd been seeking, Jack rose to his full height. An officer inside the building was ready to rush the boy if James turned the gun away from the child for even a second.

He stood.

James, startled, aimed the gun at Jack, who pushed up the window and climbed in. "Just didn't want you—"

The rest of his words were lost in the chaos that followed. A couple of officers appeared from the back of the room as Jack put himself between the boy and the small blond girl lying on the floor. With one officer on either side and others filling the back of the room, they apprehended the boy.

Jack reached for the now-hysterical child.

And a shot rang out.

CHAPTER SIX

June 1997

ERICA TRIED not to scream. To conserve energy. Panting, she rode out the pain. And wanted to die when relief finally, briefly, took its place.

"How many hours has it been?" she asked, not recognizing the hoarse voice as her own.

"Twenty-three."

Through the haze of exhaustion and bright lights, she could barely see Jefferson hovering beside her.

"Too long," she croaked. "I can't do it."

He slid an ice chip between her cracked lips. "Yes, you can."

Sucking greedily, she turned her head away from him and from the nurse who'd just appeared to check the glucose running through her IV. "I don't want to."

Not without Jack.

"Yes, you do, hon. You've been waiting for that baby a long time. Long before we knew he was a boy, before he had a name. You were talking to him. Loving him. Thinking about holding him in your arms."

Holding her baby. Oh, yeah. She'd do anything for that....

The next time the doctor told her to push, Erica squeezed her eyes shut and found the strength to focus on the little body trying to fight its way free. Her entire life force was centered on making her son's advent into life as smooth as possible. Which meant she had to work as hard as she could, as quickly as she could.

Another push. And then another. More ice chips. Jack beside her. Holding her hand. No, that was Jefferson.

The hospital garb he was wearing made her confusion a little more excusable.

Jack was inside her. In her mind, her heart, birthing their son with her. He knew nothing about the boy nor, she was certain, would he welcome the news, but she couldn't do this without him. She imagined Jack as he'd been before the tragic loss of his young family, that Jack would probably have been so actively involved in the birth of his son he'd have been a pain in the— No. He would've made Kevin's arrival perfect.

Kevin—named after his maternal grandfather. Jefferson's idea.

"That's good, honey. You're doing amazing things," Jefferson said softly beside her.

Though it took mammoth effort, Erica focused on him. And smiled. She was very lucky to have his support.

When he put the next ice chip against her lips, he leaned down and kissed her neck, almost as though he thought she'd be so distracted by the ice she wouldn't notice.

"I'm proud of you," he whispered.

"I'm proud of you, too." Her voice was dry, raspy.

"Just another push or two," Dr. Jocelyn said cheerfully from her vantage point at the end of the bed.

Erica was almost surprised to find her there. There'd been so many people in and out of her room, checking on her over the past day, that she'd long since tuned them out.

"Look, Senator, you can see your son's hair," the doctor said in the middle of the next push.

Yes. Kevin was Jefferson's son.

And no man could have been more supportive or proud or loving when Kevin Jefferson Cooley put in his appearance twenty minutes later. With the baby resting on her stomach, Erica watched through blurry eyes as Jefferson cut the umbilical cord. And then he gently placed her son in her shaking arms.

Erica, fatigue forgotten, laughed, stared at her baby, fell in love.

And silently, secretly, cried for Jack.

July 1999

SWEATING, STILL WEARING her in-line skating gear, Erica leaned against a tree in the park a couple of blocks from their condo and watched, unnoticed, as her husband and son romped in the grass just a few yards away. She could hardly believe Jefferson was still at it, patiently tossing the foam baseball to the miniature foam mitt resting precariously on the two-year-old's right hand. The fact that even after she'd skated a solid hour, Kevin was still attempting to stay on his feet and catch that ball didn't surprise her a bit.

Her son's personality was a mixture of precociousness and determination.

And her husband was the most perfect father she could imagine. Jefferson never ran out—not of patience, not of time, and not of the money it took to make sure that Kevin had the best of everything.

Even from this location she could see the puckering of her toddler's brow as he concentrated, reached and fell on his diapered behind before the ball was anywhere near his mitt. His voice was only a note on the wind, but Erica knew that he was giving Jefferson his baby rendition of "throw it again, Daddy."

"Da Da" had been the first word Kevin had said. And continued to be the most frequent.

Releasing the Velcro straps on her wrist and knee guards, Erica removed her helmet, tucked the guards inside and slid out of her skates.

She and Jefferson had a formal dinner downtown that night. It was time to get Kevin home, bathed and fed before his sitter arrived. Erica wanted to put all her remaining energy that evening into being the best wife and communications director she could, in an attempt to somehow repay her husband for the wonderful gift he was to her.

August 2000

ALONE IN THE DEN of the condo he'd shared with Erica for more than seven years, Jefferson Cooley nursed his drink, wondering how everything had gotten so mixed up. Erica was upstairs, looking beautiful as ever as she slept in their bed, dreaming, he was sure, of the man she'd known only a week and loved for more than four years.

On the surface they had a great life. His career was solid, successful. Deemed the father of stem-cell research because of the bold resolutions he'd fought to get passed through Congress, he was a hero in the eyes of his country. He was also a potential running mate for the Republican presidential ticket in another couple of years if he decided to consider the invitation.

Their condo was the envy of everyone who visited, the brown leather couch he was sitting on the best that money could buy. There was a park right outside their door where he and Kevin could play catch every evening.

Kevin. The three-year-old scrap who'd completely changed his life. The boy was the light of Jefferson's days and nights, the joy in his heart. Legs spread, elbows on his knees with his glass clasped in both hands, Jefferson hung his head. Kevin. His son, who made his life endurable—more than endurable.

And yet, while he was the best father to Kevin he knew how to be, he hadn't fathered him.

Someday the boy was going to know that. And when he did, he'd want to meet Jack Shaw—a man who'd still be young enough to tackle him when Kevin was on the high-school football team. Jefferson would be well into his seventies by then.

Kevin, his greatest blessing—and a constant reminder of his failure as a man. Not only could he not arouse his wife's passion, he wasn't capable of giving her babies to love, either.

Erica had gotten both from another man.

Swallowing another sip of the smoothest whiskey it was possible to buy, Jefferson wondered where his life had gone so wrong. Which turn had put him on this road to hell. That long-ago evening, after hours in his senatorial offices, when he'd talked Erica into marrying him?

Or had it been before that? When he'd first fallen in love with the daughter of one of his most trusted business associates?

He finished off the shot, reached for the open bottle on the table in front of him, refilled his glass and drank it in one gulp. The next shot he took a little more slowly, giving the burn that followed the trail of the liquor time to subside.

He'd made love to his wife that night. She'd come into his arms willingly, caressed him in all the places she knew he was most sensitive. She'd welcomed him inside her, loving him generously. And all out of duty. He couldn't even pretend there'd been any passion.

A quick gulp of liquor stung his throat and unaccustomed tears sprang to his eyes. He'd just made love to a very compassionate piece of cardboard. And he'd been so damn desperate for her that he'd shuddered all over her with the strength of his orgasm.

In the eyes of his country, he was a hero. In the eyes of his young wife, a pathetic old man.

When had the joy of being allowed to share Erica's life ceased to be enough? When had it started damaging what once it had blessed?

Another visit between bottle and glass. Another sip.

He was afraid to even consider what their relationship was doing to Erica. She loved him. He was in no doubt of that. As a very dear and trusted friend. A protector. A confidant. A father figure. Not as a man.

And she seemed to torture herself with guilt for that every day of their lives. The greatest irony was that the fault lay with him. He'd approached her when she was at a low point, grieving over lost dreams, lost love and hope, a lost marriage, and he'd let her convince him that she was never going to love again. He was the one with the experience, the greater wisdom, yet he'd allowed himself to be convinced of something he knew wasn't true. Erica had been too young to write herself off that way.

But rather than give her the chance to find that out, he'd married her. Ultimately he'd forced her into what would become—what *had* become—an untenable situation when she finally did discover that there was still passion in her soul.

So where did that leave them?

Sitting back on the couch, Jefferson remembered something Pamela had said to him the day before.

An attorney on his staff, she'd been discussing some ramifications of a particular bill with him. She'd pointed out how he could work things so the bill could slide past his legal team, but he'd kept at her—and the problem—to find a way to word the bill and yet still take the high moral ground.

When they'd finally succeeded, she'd told him there were very few men like him in Washington. And that it was too bad he was taken.

Though it might have sounded like flirtation, from Pamela it had been sincere.

Still, it was something he'd heard many times before.

What made this time so different was the way Pamela had said the words. As if she was personally very sorry that he was already spoken for.

She'd made him feel special in a way he hadn't felt in years. At that moment, he hadn't been a powerful senator. He hadn't been rich or famous. He'd simply been a desirable man.

It was a feeling he'd needed from his wife that night. And Erica had known. It was why she'd tried so hard. And then, when trying alone didn't work, it was why, in the end, she'd faked her response.

Jefferson sat a long time, staring off into the darkness, a strong, optimistic man who was losing faith.

Along with the dignity he'd already lost.

June 2001

TWO DAYS BEFORE Kevin's fourth birthday, excited about the party plans she'd made—all centering on the guest appearance of a friend of Jefferson's who happened to be first baseman for the Atlanta Braves—Erica breezed right by Jeff's secretary and went barreling into her husband's office.

Only to stand there shocked as Jeff and Legislative

Attorney Pamela Woods broke apart. They'd been in each other's arms.

Erica just couldn't figure out why.

"Erica!" her husband said. "Is something wrong? Is it Kevin?" His immediate concern was reassuring. Pamela's bowed head was not.

Nor, once she had a second for the thought to sink in, was the idea that Jeff assumed the only reason she'd seek him out was to discuss their son. Of course, that *was* why she'd gone to his office, she remembered with a pang of guilt.

That pang was about the only familiar thing at the moment, the only sensation she recognized.

Certainly the expression on her husband's face wasn't one she'd ever seen before. Guilt. Shame. As though he'd been caught with his hand in the till. Jefferson was the most honest, upright man she'd ever met. Which made him a bit of an anachronism in this town of fast talk and even faster moves.

Erica's thoughts were coming in slow motion as she stood there. She didn't speak. She didn't laugh. Or cry. She didn't do a single thing.

His hand hadn't been in the till. Unless she'd been mistaken, Jeff's hand had been inside Ms. Woods's suit jacket. Right at breast level.

"Erica," Jeff said, his voice filled with contrition. And perhaps pity. "Say something."

No. This wasn't happening. It couldn't be happening. No. She shook her head for good measure.

"I'm sorry," Jeff said.

The tone of his voice, the depth of sorrow, cut

through the fog surrounding her. He was hurting her. More than she'd ever thought possible.

Because she wasn't in love with Jefferson, she was supposed to be protected from ever feeling this kind of pain again.

"I'd better go." Pamela's soft words registered, but Erica couldn't have acknowledged them if she'd wanted to.

She didn't think she wanted to.

"Jeff?" she cried as soon as she heard the door close behind the attractive older woman.

He didn't say anything. Just wrapped those strong, dependable arms around her and held on.

"I'm so sorry, honey," he said.

"Sorry for doing it? Or sorry I found out?" she asked, the words muffled against his shirt.

"I'm sorry I hurt you." He had a third choice. "Especially like this."

Yeah, she was pretty damn sorry, too.

But she deserved it. After what she'd done to Jeff almost five years before, she had no right to be upset at finding her husband in the arms of another woman. Hell, she and Jack had been in a hotel room. Eventually in bed. Jeff had just been standing fully clothed in his office...

"It's not the first time, is it?" she whispered.

"No."

"Have you slept with her?"

"Not yet."

Not yet. As though he planned to.

That knife stabbed so sharply she couldn't breathe. For a second there, the world spun. She couldn't go on. Couldn't move forward. Or away. She couldn't go through this again.

Jefferson was her best friend. He loved her. Desperately.

And, in her way, she loved him, too. But not in the *same* way...

She caught her breath. And then lost it again on a painful hiccup that, had she been some other woman, might have turned into a sob. For Erica, it settled into a suffocating tightness inside her. Hidden. Scary.

Because she didn't know what else to do, she stood there and let him hold her, let him rub her rigid back.

"How long?" She finally mustered the question, though its significance was lost on her.

"A while."

Eventually Erica pulled away and walked over to the leather couch in Jeff's office. She'd fallen asleep there just last week, comforted, after a grueling day, by the sound of her husband's calm voice while he completed a late conference call. She'd been waiting for him to finish so they could go home together, have dinner with Kevin, tuck him in.

Wishing she was a weaker woman, she sat down calmly, as though she could handle anything. She would rather have fallen apart, let Jeff take care of her. Because then she might be able to prevent what she feared was coming next.

"We need to get a divorce, honey."

It came.

He sat close beside her, sliding one arm across her shoulders.

"You've been eating yourself alive for years over the fact that you can't make yourself fall in love with me...."

Pulling out of his embrace far enough to be able to look him in the eye, Erica said, "I love you, Jeff. Very much."

If she could, she'd open her heart and show him he really did belong there.

"I know you do," he said, his gaze implacable. "Like a father, maybe, or an older uncle. But you're *in* love with someone else."

"No," Erica said, not recognizing the frightened quality in the voice she heard. She shook her head. "I haven't seen Jack or even heard from him. Not once in all these years." She took a deep breath. "I've never looked back, Jefferson, I swear to you. From the moment I told you what I'd done, from the moment you forgave me, I've been faithful to you."

"In body," he said, trailing a finger along her creased brow. "But not in your heart, Erica. The memory of that man burns there."

"We don't need to divorce, Jeff. I don't want to divorce. I'm happy being married to you."

"You've settled for being married to me."

"I give everything I've got to you."

"To me and Kevin," he said. And then, "I know you do, Erica, but you aren't happy, not deep down, where it matters most."

"I—"

He put one finger against her lips. "And I'm not happy, either."

"But you said that sharing my life was the thing you wanted most in the world."

"It used to be. Until it started to rob me of self-respect."

"I don't understand." But she did.

Jeff sat back, pulling her with him, running his fingers through the short wisps of her hair as she settled her head against his chest. The position was comforting. Familiar.

This was her husband. Things would work out. They always did.

They had to.

"I might be looking at seventy just a few years down the road, but I still need to feel like a desirable man."

"We can make love more often…"

"I make love," he corrected. "You love me by allowing me to do so."

"I—"

"Don't cheapen what we have with anything less than total honesty." He'd never spoken to her in that tone before. "We both know I don't arouse passion in you."

"But—"

"I need passion, Erica."

He was right. Everything he'd said was right. Erica felt sick. "And that woman gives you…passion?"

"Yes."

"And you want to lose everything we've built over the years, everything good that we share, for a little *passion?*" She wasn't being fair and she knew it.

"No, if it was just the passion, probably not. But it's more than that. It's not even about Pamela."

"What then?"

"It has to do with what she's taught me about myself. Years of living with a woman who doesn't desire him, of bearing the heavier part of an unequal love, can be…damaging to a man's self-esteem."

She had to sit up. To separate herself from him. Set them both free. But she couldn't move. "I make you feel bad about yourself."

She'd wondered. And had tried so hard to prevent that.

"Probably as bad as not being in love with me makes *you* feel about yourself," he said. "I see the guilt in your eyes when we make love and you don't come," he said. "Or worse, when you pretend to."

What a blind fool she'd been to hope he hadn't noticed.

"You're only thirty-seven, honey. You still have a whole life of love and passion ahead of you. I can't go on depriving you of that chance."

If he'd been anyone but Jefferson, Erica would've suspected she was being fed a line, that he really wanted his freedom so he could screw his girlfriend. But this was Jeff. He always put others' needs—especially hers—above his own.

"You don't love me anymore?" She hated that she even asked. But while he was right—she didn't love him the way a woman was supposed to love her husband—she *did* care about Jefferson. Cared about him deeply.

"Of course I love you." His voice caught and he

pulled her tightly against him. "It's because I love you that I know we have to do this."

"You want to marry Pamela."

"Maybe, but while she's certainly been a catalyst in my decision, I've known for a couple of years that I had to let you go."

She believed him. And believed that he still loved her.

And because she cared for him, far more than he realized, Erica had to let him go, too.

"Okay," she said.

The room was silent after that. Tuning in to Jefferson's steady heartbeat, absorbing the warmth from his body, Erica tried to keep panic at bay. To find something she could hold on to.

"You aren't firing me, too, are you?"

"Of course not! I'd be lost without you."

Like a break between harsh labor pains, Erica's anxiety calmed for a second. She would still see Jefferson every day, still be part of his life. She could do this.

"What about Kevin?" she asked

"Obviously he stays with you."

Obviously. That wasn't what she'd meant. "He adores you."

"I assume I'll still be seeing him every day. Taking him to ball games. Keeping his life as much the same as possible."

"Just not sleeping with his mother."

Neither of them mentioned that Jefferson didn't do that much anymore. He worked late in the den, then stayed in the guest room if she was already asleep.

Neither of them said anything at all for a long time. Still, she lay cuddled against his chest. She didn't want to move. Didn't ever want to move.

Except that their son was waiting for them. In a matter of minutes she'd have to find the strength to pretend that her world hadn't just come crashing down.

"You're going to be fine."

"Yeah."

But she wasn't.

Thinking about life without Jefferson, all she could feel was exhaustion.

And a pain so intense she couldn't imagine ever recovering.

CHAPTER SEVEN

May 2002

ERICA'S LIFE was defined by paradox. At work, as communications director, she was responsible for putting a positive spin on Jefferson's divorce. She was his advocate, his cheering squad. And once again she did a damn good job for him. Six months after their quiet divorce, Jefferson was as high in the polls as he'd been after Kevin was born.

At home, though, she was the woman trying to cope with his defection. He'd promised always to be there for her. To protect her from the betrayal. He'd promised her constancy and fidelity and then changed his mind. It was worse the second time around.

And everywhere, her divorce was the most talked-about paradox. Instead of leaving the older woman who'd stood beside him through the hard times, who'd helped him get to the top, her politician ex-husband had left a beautiful, young wife for a woman his own age.

"Hey, Mom, that looks like a good spot, don't you

think? That patch right there under the—'' he looked up, thought a minute ''—elm tree.''

Looking where her almost five-year-old son's finger was pointing, Erica nodded. ''Good eye, sport.''

They were on Capitol Hill this beautiful May Thursday, looking for a spot to eat the sandwiches she'd just bought them for lunch. The big grassy area in front of the Capitol Building was close to the Cooley offices in the Hart Senate Office Building and one of Kevin's favorite places to hang out. She'd worn her navy silk business suit today, just for the occasion. The one with slacks. Her skirts made it a little hard to accommodate a young boy's yearning for picnics.

Quite often, like today, when Erica knew she didn't have any meetings scheduled, she'd bring Kevin to work with her. He was a favorite around the office, everyone fighting over who got to ''visit'' with him, and he loved to watch his mother and father at work. Since Jefferson had moved out of their condo and wasn't there to have breakfast with them, Erica liked to give Kevin any extra time she could around his father.

Jeff had been planning to share their lunch, but the morning session had run late.

''Oh, fudge,'' Kevin muttered, looking like a miniature Capitol Hill-ite himself in his dark slacks, white shirt and striped tie. ''That man's gonna take our spot.''

''No, he's not,'' Erica said, smiling at her far-too-mature little boy. ''He's walking with too much purpose to stop under a tree.''

In truth, she hardly noticed the man, intent as she was on her contemplation of life—of her ex-husband in meetings with a roomful of people that happened to include Pamela Woods—and of the pure joy she found in the small boy at her side.

"Yes, he is, Mom. Look!" Kevin said. "We better hurry. That's the only place left with shade, and you know you like shade." The words sounded like those of a nagging teenager.

Erica followed her five-year-old's orders. She looked. And her steps faltered. It had been more than five years, and she was still seeing Jack in strange men on the street. Or in this case, the grass of Capitol Hill.

Holding the brown bag full of chips and condiments that had come with the sandwiches, Kevin strode ahead, glancing back at her with a frown when she didn't immediately fall into step with him.

To please her son, Erica sped up. But she slowed again as they drew closer to their destination. The man who was walking toward them bore an uncanny resemblance to Jack Shaw.

A resemblance that seemed to grow rather than dissipate the nearer he came. Erica started to search for the differences.

"Come on, Mo-o-o-om." Kevin might have stomped his little wing-tipped shoe if he'd thought he could get away with it.

The man's dark-blond hair was touched with gray. He was a little thinner than Jack. But the walk was exactly the same. A little slower than most people's, as though he had all the time in the world to reach his destination—and yet confident, as though he knew exactly where he was going and how to get there.

He missed a step. Seemed to be staring at her.

"He's taking the spot, Mom! Your shade." The little boy stopped, the threat of tears in his voice.

"It's okay, Kev," she said softly, her gaze never moving from the man standing under their tree, watching her.

"Erica?" His voice was just as it had been in her dream a couple of nights before.

"Jack." His name sounded more like a croak; she cleared her throat and tried again. "Jack."

The people milling around them on Capitol Hill—important people trying to change the world, homeless people, tourists with mouths agape taking pictures—all faded away.

Do something, you idiot, she thought as she stood there staring. But she didn't do anything. Just stood. And stared. A human land mine waiting to be detonated.

She was so cold.

And she was hot.

Jack was here. Right here where she could touch him. She was afraid that if she moved, she'd break into hysterical laughter—or tears. Almost six years. That was a long time to be away from someone you'd connected with as intensely as Erica had with Jack.

"This was *our* spot." Kevin stood by his mother, looking up at the stranger with complete unselfconsciousness.

Oh, no.

Kevin. And Jack. Father and son.

She'd completely forgotten about her son. About the significance of his presence. Used to smoothing over awkward situations, Erica didn't often find herself at a complete loss. She had no idea what to do.

"It's, uh, okay, sport, we'll go somewhere...else." She stumbled through what was supposed to be an upbeat, natural-sounding response.

"No need, I'm not staying," Jack said. "I have a report to pick up across the street." But he didn't leave.

Part of her was aware of Kevin looking from one to the other, his small brow creased.

She couldn't believe Jack was actually here, standing in front of her, as though this happened regularly. She'd never seen him in slacks and a tie. He'd never seen his son.

Kevin stepped closer to Erica, sliding his free hand into hers. "Do you know this man, Mom?" he asked, his tone as protective as an almost five-year-old's could get. "Does he work with Daddy? I've never seen him before."

When her numb brain considered the paradox of those last words—Kevin had never seen Jack, his father—a flash of intense sadness shot through her.

"I do know him, Kev, yes," she said in the best mommy voice she could muster. "But he doesn't work with Daddy. He's an old friend of Mommy's."

"Oh." The boy considered Jack.

Jack hadn't said a word. Hands in his pockets, one knee casually bent, he watched Erica, and then, with partially lowered lids, took in Kevin for a long moment.

Dropping Erica's hand, Kevin thrust out his palm. "Hi, I'm Kevin," he said.

Without missing a beat, Jack took the hand her son—his son—offered, shaking it, without understanding the relevance of what he was doing.

But Erica knew. And started to cry inside.

"Hi, Kevin, I'm Jack."

"What do you do?" Kevin asked, small arms folded across his chest, his brown bag full of chips dangling awkwardly.

"I used to work for the FBI."

Kevin nodded. "I know some people who work there," he said.

Smiling at the boy, Jack's eyes rose to meet Erica's once again. And the look in those eyes took her breath away. For that brief second, they weren't in Washington, D.C., standing on Capitol Hill with their son between them. They were back in New York City, in a hotel room....

"He's your son." Jack said the words she couldn't.

"Yes." She needed a sip from one of the bottles of water in the bag she was carrying. Her throat was dry.

"I read that you and Jefferson had him, what—four years ago?"

Greedily she took the out he'd unknowingly presented. "He's four, yes."

If she told him that Kevin was going to be five the next month, would it give him pause?

But she couldn't. Now more than ever, Kevin was Jefferson's son. She'd chosen Jack over loyalty to Jefferson once before. She couldn't do that again.

She also knew, in that split second of unreality, that Kevin needed her to keep her secret more than anyone else did. Her son was still trying to adjust to the changes in his life brought about by the divorce. She couldn't upset his precarious hold on emotional stability with more life-changing news.

In the past six months Kevin had aged thirty years. He'd gone from toddler to adult when Jefferson moved out. She'd taken him to a psychiatrist. She and Jefferson had both worked with him incessantly, and still, this tiny man remained where the little boy had once lived.

"I also read that you and Jefferson divorced."

He was keeping better track of Washington politicians these days. "Yeah. It was final six months ago."

"I'm sorry." The compassion in those eyes, the quiet intimacy of that look, tormented her. She just had to hold on a few more seconds and this would be over. He had someplace to go.

"Daddy and Mom are still best friends," Kevin said, interrupting their silent exchange. "He comes home from work and has dinner with us most of the nights." His small features were heartbreaking in their earnestness.

"You're still working for him, too," Jack said.

She didn't want him to walk away.

"Yeah."

He nodded, connecting with her through looks more than words.

"Was the divorce really your idea like the papers said?" he asked abruptly.

"No."

"I didn't think so."

That surprised her. Considering that he was the only other person alive who knew how thoroughly she'd betrayed her husband, she would've expected him to assume that she was indeed responsible for the termination of her marriage.

Kevin, whose hair was the same dark blond shade as that of the man standing there delaying their lunch, took the bag from his mother's hand. "I'm hungry. Can we eat now?"

"Of course, honey," Erica said, smiling at him, loving him, more thankful than she could ever express that he was hers, blessing her life.

Kevin was what mattered.

"Would you like a sandwich, too?" he asked Jack. "We bought one for Daddy, but he won't be here today."

Jack had begun to shake his head, but he stopped when he heard about the rejection the boy had already received, arching his brows as he looked at Erica. "Thanks, I'd like that," Jack said. And then to Erica, "Does he do that a lot?"

"Who?"

Jack was staying. Her son had bought her a few more minutes. Erica was elated. And worried. She needed him to go.

"Jefferson. Does he miss dates with the boy?"

"Almost never. My meeting was canceled this morning so I decided to bring Kevin at the last minute. Jefferson tried to finish up in time, but with so little notice..."

"Okay, we're eating now, right, Mom?" Kevin asked, dropping to his knees on the grass. He dug into the bag with all the finesse of a hungry little boy. His childish enthusiasm was a relief.

"Right," she said, wondering how on earth she was going to sit here with her son and her son's father and take a single bite of anything. She was ready to explode with what she knew about these two people she cared about so much.

What she knew and what *they* didn't know. Three words, and all their lives would change forever.

He's your son.

Three words she could never say.

"Well, you sit here, Mom," Kevin said, pointing to one side of him. "And you sit here." He plopped Jack's paper-wrapped sandwich down in the grass. "And here's waters." He tried to stand the bottles in the grass. When they fell over, he tried again, only giving up after a third try. "And chips, too."

He missed the napkins that were also in the bag.

Erica sat down with an awkwardness that was a sacrilege to the memories she carried of her and Jack—memories of their naturalness together, their ease. And somehow made it through the next ten minutes as her son, with crumbs and a smear of mayonnaise on his face, virtually besieged her ex-lover with questions about his time with the FBI.

"Did you know my daddy's a senator?" Kevin

asked suddenly. Only the crusts of his sandwich were left, carefully placed on the paper wrap in front of him.

Jack had finished his sandwich, as well. Crusts and all. "Yes, I did," he told Kevin.

"He works right over there." The boy pointed at the Hart Senate Office Building.

"I hear he's pretty important," Jack said. He hadn't looked at Erica since they'd sat down.

For which she was thankful. Left alone, she'd managed to eat enough of her sandwich to keep Kevin from noticing that something was wrong.

Kevin handed Jack two bags of chips. "He *is* important," he said in a matter-of-fact tone. "He's a hero, you know, 'cause of stem cells and other stuff. Here's yours. Can you open mine, too?"

Jack opened the bags. "I'd like to meet him sometime," he told the boy, passing back his chips.

Jack was just being kind to Kevin in saying that he'd like to meet his daddy, but Erica couldn't think of anything worse than Jack and Jefferson in the same room. The man she'd betrayed. And the man she'd betrayed him with.

Self-loathing robbed her of any remaining appetite.

DAMN, IT WAS GOOD to see her. Too good probably. Dumping their trash in the nearest receptacle, Jack walked with Erica and her son across the lawn to the National Mall, although it was in the opposite direction from where he needed to go.

She'd promised the boy a few minutes in one of

the museums before going back to the office. And he wasn't ready to say goodbye just yet.

He'd been to the Capitol a few times over the years. Each time he'd had to fight with himself not to call her. After the news of her divorce, the fight had grown more fierce. But the reasons for not doing it stayed the same. Jack wasn't going to let anyone get close enough to change his life. Not again.

Each internal fight had eventually ended with the same compromise. He'd talk to her if he ran into her. Like a besotted fool, he'd watched every woman he'd passed on those visits, but he'd never run into her.

Until now.

As they reached the huge expanse of grass that ran along the center of the National Mall, Kevin darted ahead of them, lost in some game of his own making. Jack had no idea what it was, only that it involved hopping on one leg. And looked like fun. Even in the restrictive clothes he was wearing.

"He's sure the little senator," he said, watching the boy. Though he went cold at the thought of having a child of his own, he was glad Erica had Kevin. He liked to think of her with that kind of love in her life.

She shrugged, as quiet as she'd been during lunch. "He's Jefferson's son through and through," she said. "I see Jeff's mannerisms in almost everything Kevin does."

"He looks like you."

She stumbled, her high heel catching in the grass, but caught herself before Jack could steady her.

"People say that," she said. "But I don't see it. He looks like…his father to me."

Since he'd never seen Jefferson Cooley except on television, and then, only once or twice, Jack couldn't really judge the accuracy of that.

What he could judge, though, was Erica. It had been almost six years, of course, but she'd changed a lot. It wasn't just the sadness in her eyes or the lack of bounce in her step. It was the distance she seemed to be putting between her and the world. Between the two of them.

"It's great to see you," he said, thinking he should've come up with a more original remark. Or at least a more significant one.

"You, too."

She didn't look at him.

Jack had to get over to the Capitol Building. He had a meeting in twenty minutes and needed the report he was supposed to have picked up almost an hour ago.

Yet the same thing that had drawn him to her all those years ago in New York drew him again. She'd never really left his thoughts…or his dreams.

"Are you free for dinner?" Probably not a good idea. But he couldn't just walk away. Not without finding out what was making her so unhappy. Not without seeing if there was something he could do to help before he went back to his own life.

Her only answer was silence.

With a hand on her wrist, he stopped her, waiting until she finally looked at him before continuing,

"I'd really like a chance to catch up on the past few years," he said. "I've missed you."

She closed her eyes.

"One night, for old times' sake," he said.

"Okay." Her lids raised slowly. He read the doubt in her eyes. And worse, the wariness.

"Really?" Based on the impressions he was getting, he felt surprised as hell that she'd agreed.

"Yes." She nodded. "I'll have Jeff take Kevin home with him. We can meet here in town and go to the Prime Rib, if that's all right with you."

"Great," he said quickly. The forties-style supper club was a good choice. Public enough to keep them safe, comfortable enough to allow for a long visit. He was staying at an apartment close by—owned by a buddy of his from the bureau whose main residence was in Virginia—and could easily walk to the restaurant. "Seven okay with you?"

"Fine. I'll meet you there. I'll look forward to it."

Hands in his pockets, Jack called goodbye to Kevin, who was still hopping and now waving an arm oddly, as well, and headed back in the direction they'd come, wishing it was seven o'clock already.

Erica had said she was looking forward to the evening, too, but she wasn't letting Jack anywhere near any of her real thoughts and feelings. He wasn't going to rest until he found out why.

CHAPTER EIGHT

SHE SHOULD HAVE chosen a different place to meet him. Sitting in the black leather chair at the impeccably set table, waiting for Jack, Erica looked around for anyone she knew. The Prime Rib was a hot spot among Washington's elite, a real insiders' favorite. She'd been aiming for the safety and comfort afforded by familiarity. She hadn't considered the discomfort created by the presence of curious acquaintances.

Just being in this place, meeting Jack where she and Jefferson had done so much business over the years, made her feel guilty as hell.

Only the fact that Kevin and Jefferson were at the condo, playing catch and having some much-needed guy-time, appeased her conscience enough to allow her to stay. All she wanted to do was find out that Jack's life was going well. That he was okay.

She saw him the minute he walked in the door. Heart quickening, she watched him speak to the maître d' and then cross the room. Unlike many of the politicians, lawyers and lobbyists who'd come straight from work, herself included, he'd changed clothes. He was wearing navy slacks and a light-blue oxford shirt with a navy-and-white-striped tie. His jacket, required dress at the Prime Rib, was a navy tweed.

Full of emotion, she didn't say a word as he took the seat across from her.

"I'm glad you're here," he told her, his smile slow in coming. "I thought you might change your mind, and then I realized I'd given you no way to reach me."

"I had to come."

The look in his eyes shifted, wariness giving way to intimacy. Before he could say anything, their waiter appeared, welcoming them, taking Jack's order for a shot of whiskey on the rocks and hers for a glass of wine.

Exactly what they'd been drinking the last time they were together. That night in her hotel room...

"Just like old times, huh?" he asked.

Erica smiled, blushed, but she couldn't decide how to respond, so she said nothing. She hated being so unsure of herself.

"I've missed you."

The warmth in his voice, the expression on his face, suggested that not only could he see inside her, but really liked what he saw there. Everything about him was as compelling as it had been almost six years before.

"I've missed you, too. A lot." There. It felt better to have acknowledged some real feeling. So maybe that was what this evening would be. A time for expressing emotions. Releasing them.

Saying goodbye?

Their drinks came. They ordered dinner. Entrées, not the appetizers they'd settled for at Maggie's Place that week in New York. But then, the Prime Rib, with its formal decor and live soft jazz piano music, was about as different from Maggie's as you could get.

It was one of the reasons she'd chosen the place.

Erica ordered the Chesapeake rockfish stuffed with crab. Jack chose the porterhouse steak, a twenty-four-ounce cut of premium filet mignon and prime sirloin. He wasn't a seafood person. She hadn't known that.

Feeling awkward, Erica realized that although she'd made a baby with this man, she'd never even had a meal with him. A few appetizers, but never an actual meal. She knew what kind of lover he was, but knew nothing about his food likes and dislikes. She knew how to please him in bed, but wouldn't know the first thing about preparing a breakfast that he'd like.

It made their time in New York seem cheap.

And yet, looking across the candlelit table at him, she knew it hadn't been.

"You look good," she told him.

"Thanks." He paused, glanced down and then back across at her, his eyes taking on a glint from the candlelight. "You're more beautiful than ever, of course, but you don't look happy."

She shrugged. "I'm adjusting."

"The divorce."

"Yes." An ability to say anything had been one of the defining characteristics of that week in New York.

He sat back, ankle resting across his knee, arms on the armrests, his drink between his hands.

"Had you seen it coming?"

Shaking her head once, Erica picked up her wine, took a sip. "I had no idea. I thought we were happy…"

Compared to what she'd felt since the divorce, they had been.

"…but Jefferson said I was settling."

"Were you?"

"Probably, but I didn't have a problem with that." She'd had no trouble getting out of bed in the mornings, had looked forward to each day. "Jeff and I had always been good together, and adding Kevin to the mix made it near perfect, as far as I was concerned."

She'd had everything she wanted. And none of what she didn't want. She'd had someone she cared about to come home to, someone to share life's fortunes and challenges. And none of the devitalizing vulnerability—the risk—she'd experienced with her first marriage.

"I really worked hard to make sure Jeff had what he needed. Making him happy was my priority. Especially after…"

She should have looked away from those compelling eyes. But she couldn't, any more than she could have walked out of the restaurant at this moment.

"After New York," he finished softly.

She nodded. Needed to look around, to see who else was in the room with them, to reassure herself that someone *was* there, that they weren't in a world all their own.

Why did it always seem that way with her and Jack? As though they existed in their own private sphere, speaking a language no one else could hear or understand.

"So he just came to you one day and told you it was over?" His tone was compassionate.

"No." She looked away then, couldn't let him see the depth of her shame. Couldn't bear to have him know her that intimately, to be that close. "I walked in on him and his girlfriend."

Jack's glass landed on the table with a thud, his expletive leaving her no doubt that in him she still had a champion.

Not that that meant anything in a practical sense.

"The man robs the cradle and he still can't stay faithful?" Jack asked. "He's got a wife who's twenty-seven years younger than he is and that's not enough? What'd he do, go for thirty this time?"

"No," Erica actually smiled. And then, taking another sip of wine, she shook her head. They were both ignoring the salads that had been placed before them. Apparently Jack had missed the majority of the carefully orchestrated press about her and Jefferson. "Pamela's only a few years younger than Jeff."

"Oh." He sat back. Picked up his glass.

"How humiliating is that?" she asked, trying to make light of feelings she really didn't understand well enough to come to terms with. "Instead of the older wife being left by the rich successful husband she'd sacrificed her younger years to help, Jeff leaves his young wife for an older woman." She didn't mention that she herself had created the PR campaign encouraging the nation to believe in exactly this scenario.

Jack didn't say anything for a while. Just studied her.

She started in on her salad.

"You blame yourself."

She looked up, fork in hand. She should've known he'd understand. "Who else is there to blame?" It wasn't as if this was the first time it had happened to her. Both times she'd been complacent, happy, unaware. "I have a tendency not to realize when I'm not making people happy."

"Or maybe you've just married the wrong men."

God, she hated the sound of that. *Men.* Plural. She'd been through not one, but two unsuccessful marriages. She'd never envisioned herself as a woman who'd have multiple husbands. Exactly the opposite. She'd always believed in happily ever after. Had been so certain she'd have the same kind of marriage her parents had. A long, loving, supportive life together that lasted until "death do you part."

"YOU SAID YOU HAD a meeting today," Erica said as she scooped up a bite of the mashed potatoes she'd ordered with her fish. "Were you working on a job? Someone here in town was being held hostage?"

Jack didn't answer her right away. He cut a piece of steak, took a sip of Scotch. He knew he was slowing his time with her as much as possible. He thought he'd blown out of proportion his memories of how good it had been to be with Erica Cooley. At least expected their distinctive connection to have dissipated over the years.

It hadn't.

"I'm not here on a hostage case," he told her, leaving the bite of steak waiting at the end of his fork. "I've been asked to head up a new crisis-training center here in the city. It's not just for law-enforcement officials. It'll also be made available to companies who want to send upper-management personnel. Individuals can attend, as well. With the way the world has changed in the past decade, especially in the past year, it's become apparent that there's a need for more mass preparation." He ate the piece of steak.

"You're moving to Washington?"

Erica glanced up, but only briefly. Not long enough for Jack to gauge her reaction to the idea.

Would it matter to her to have him close? Did he want it to?

It wasn't a new thought, but one he'd been considering since the Washington job offer had come in more than a month ago. In fact, his first thoughts had been of Erica—even before he found out what the job actually entailed. There'd been no doubt in his mind that he wanted her to welcome the idea as much as he'd welcomed the possibility of getting to know her on a day-to-day, real-life basis.

And then he'd remembered that he *didn't* want that. More, that she didn't come unencumbered. Erica had a son. A precocious little boy who was a huge part of her life. He'd read about Kevin's birth in the paper years ago as the popular sixty-year-old Senator Cooley introduced his first child to the world.

A child. It was enough to give him serious pause. He didn't ever want a committed relationship with a woman again. Caring for a child was even more intolerable. He couldn't do it; he'd drive both the mother and child away with his incessant hovering, his attempts to make sure the world didn't harm them. He'd be too protective. Too possessive. On the verge of neurotic.

If you'd experienced things that didn't happen to most people, you tended to overcompensate. It was an effect that couldn't be avoided.

"I haven't accepted the position yet," he finally admitted.

"Because you'd have to leave fieldwork?"

"Partially, although I wouldn't leave it entirely. I'd still be on call for certain situations."

"Like the ones involving children?"

She knew him well. They'd been together only a week and she could read him as though they'd been together for a lifetime.

In New York, a time that had a clear beginning and end, no possible entanglements, that had been a thrilling sensation—the feeling that you were the complete focus of someone's attention, that your needs and wants were identified, understood...

He returned abruptly to the present.

"Those situations and others where, for one reason or another, I might be the best choice."

Erica cut a piece of fish with her fork, raised it to her mouth, closed her lips around it, chewed, swallowed.

"Do you want the job?" she asked.

"I'm tempted when I think about the greater number of lives I can help save. Instead of one man fighting for one life at a time, we'd be preparing hundreds of people to save what could amount to thousands of lives."

"Why do I get the feeling there's more to this?"

Jack took another bite of steak. Chewed. Glanced around for their waiter. He needed a refill on his drink. And then heard himself admit something to her that he hadn't really admitted to himself yet. "I'm getting a little burned out handling nothing but crises. After a while it's hard to see good in the world when all you deal with is the bad."

"But when you rescue someone successfully..."

He looked across at her, recognized the same warmth he'd felt in New York. The warmth that had driven him to seek her out every single evening that week and, ultimately, to stay with her far longer than he should have that last night. He'd been largely responsible for the fact that she'd let herself down in such an unforgivable way.

"The successes are the reason I wouldn't give it up entirely."

"Have you had many failures?" Her voice was soft, filled with empathy.

"I haven't lost a hostage."

His whiskey was delivered. Picking up the wine bottle on their table, Jack refilled her glass. It was only her second. She was drinking more slowly these days.

"But you've lost a hostage-taker?"

"One." He found himself telling her about the young man in the Arizona high school. James Talmadge. Dinner forgotten, he sipped on the well-aged whiskey as the memories came flooding back. Visions he'd refused to see ever since the night he'd left that Arizona town. They'd been locked away for more than five years, apparently only waiting for Erica.

"Where were you when the officers were approaching him on either side?" Erica asked when he paused in the telling, her lovely brow creased beneath that sassy dark hair.

Had she been Melissa, he'd have lied to protect her.

Now he lived his life without commitments or responsibilities; it meant he didn't have to make apologies for the dangers inherent in his job. Once that changed, he wouldn't be free to do the work he needed to do.

"Standing between James and the child."

She didn't flinch. "So what happened?"

"With me as a shield, they quickly passed the little girl out the window…"

"And?"

"James shot himself."

Erica's fingers sliding over his hand brought him back from the memory of the young man lying on the floor in a pool of his own blood. He could still taste the bitterness of a wasted life. He hadn't been able to escape it for weeks afterward.

He couldn't help himself from turning his hand over and linking his fingers with hers. "I learned something that day that I'd lost sight of."

"What?" Her eyes were wide, letting him see all of her, feel all of her, as he had that long-ago week in New York.

"That the hostage-taker's life is just as important to me as the victim's. I'd been so busy concentrating on the child that I'd failed to be aware of James's state of mind, to foresee all the possibilities."

"Can you really expect that of yourself?"

He could and did. There was simply no other choice.

"SO TELL ME about your son." They'd moved on to dessert, a piece of homemade key lime pie they were sharing.

Things had become confusing to Jack. He figured bringing her son into the conversation would take care of that.

"He's a great kid," she said. Her fork was staying a safe distance from his on the plate. "He's curious about everything, loves to learn, watch cartoons and play baseball."

"I remember playing baseball as a kid," Jack said. He rarely thought back to the days of his childhood, rarely thought back to any time before Melissa's death. Because everything led to that moment in the van, when a single shot from a teenager's gun took two lives he'd sworn to protect.

"Did you play on a team?"

"Oh, yeah," he said, grinning. They were getting closer to the center of the pie. "Little League, high school, even college."

Erica raised her brows. "Sounds like you were good. What position did you play?"

He'd been scouted by the New York Yankees farm team. He'd chosen to go to the FBI Academy in Quantico, Virginia, instead, and hadn't regretted the decision even once.

His fork bumped into hers. Their eyes met. "First base."

"I'm impressed."

Jack didn't know what was happening. Didn't know what he wanted. About the only thing he felt certain of was that neither one of them was thinking about baseball.

"I DON'T WANT this to be the last time I see you."

Erica's stomach twisted and she looked away. She and Jack were standing outside the Prime Rib. Her condo was just a couple of blocks away and she was planning to walk there alone. She didn't want him to know where she lived. Didn't want to know that he knew. Because if he did, she might start wishing he'd show up there someday. Might start waiting...

"Can I call you?" he pressed.

She nodded.

Hands in his pockets, he faced her. "I'll need your number, then."

Scrambling in her purse, wondering what the hell she was doing, she took out a business card and handed it to him.

He stared at it for a minute, then caught and held her gaze. "This is your office."

Nodding again, Erica said, "It's the easiest place to reach me."

He didn't question her decision. At least not verbally.

"We live separate lives." The words were torn from her.

It was his turn to look away, but he didn't stay away long. "I know," he said, pulling her against a corner of the building as a crowd of businessmen left the restaurant and passed close to them.

"What we had in New York...it won't work in real life."

"I know."

"So why not just keep it what it was?" She could

feel tears burning behind her lids. Tears he'd never see. She was so tired.

"And what's that?"

"An incredible memory."

She could stare up at him forever. Jack was so handsome he took her breath away. But more, the vitality emanating from him enclosed her in a safe world she didn't want to leave.

"What if it's more than just a memory?" he asked.

"What if it isn't?"

"Wouldn't it be easier to find out, one way or the other?"

She wasn't so sure. Those New York memories had seen her through some of her darkest times. "There were reasons New York couldn't last more than one week," she reminded him. "They're still there."

"You aren't married anymore."

But she still cared about Jefferson, still felt a need to atone for what she'd done to him. She couldn't give him what he deserved, but he had her loyalty. It meant a lot to him. And to her. "I have a son." They both knew that was more than he'd ever be able to take on. And yet, her heart fell when he remained silent, accepting her unspoken challenge that Kevin was a problem.

"And while you might be in the field a lot less, there'll still be times when you'd have to make decisions like the one you made with James. Would you be able to do that, put your life on the line if you knew I was here, waiting for you to come home?''

"Probably. Maybe not.''

Heart pounding, Erica studied him. "Are you saying your reasons for remaining unattached no longer exist?''

She had the distinct feeling that he wanted to tell her they didn't.

"No. I can't ever be involved again to the extent that I was with Melissa. The risk is more than I'm willing to accept.''

"So...''

He leaned his forehead against hers. "I don't want this to be the last time I see you,'' he whispered.

"I don't want it to be the last time I see you, either.'' Erica licked lips that were suddenly dry.

He was going to kiss her. With her rational self, she knew it. But physically she was in denial until she felt that confident, intimate touch. The one she'd been dreaming about...

The one she'd tried not to remember every single time Jefferson had reached for her in the past six years.

Completely oblivious to where she was, to the people milling about as they left the restaurant, Erica fell back against the wall behind her, opening her lips to his.

She was thirty-two again. Believing in the possibility of a love she'd turned her back on six years before. Needy. Needing Jack.

When his tongue touched hers, he groaned and

pulled back. "Come on," he said, "I'll walk you home."

"No." Erica stepped away from the wall, away from him, her face averted. "I'll be fine by myself."

"Erica..."

She met his eyes, resolute. "I need to keep some objectivity." She told him the truth. She knew it was the only thing that was going to satisfy him.

"It's dark."

"I've walked this route many times. It's only a couple of blocks." That was more information than she'd wanted to give him.

He didn't give in easily, but he did eventually nod. Truth be known, she didn't want to be left any more than he wanted to leave her.

"I'll call you," he said, before turning to head in the opposite direction.

Erica looked back once during that first block. Jack was standing just beyond the entrance to the restaurant, watching her go.

CHAPTER NINE

JEFFERSON SAT BACK in the new green silk chair, part of the ensemble that had replaced the leather furniture he'd taken with him when he'd moved out, and watched his life play before his eyes. He'd poured himself a scotch. It was sitting on the cherry end table beside him.

Kevin was asleep in his room down the hall. Had been for more than an hour. Jefferson could have called their regular baby-sitter, a girl who lived in the building, to come and stay with the boy until Erica got home.

He was sure Erica expected him to do that. He wasn't sure why he hadn't.

Not even when he heard her key in the lock and knew she'd be wondering why he was still there.

"Hi," he said from his seat in the dark. The wall of floor-to-ceiling windows in front of him over-looked the city. The myriad lights in the cityscape were comforting.

"Jefferson?" She came into the room, dropping her purse on the Victorian sideboard on her way in. Whenever Erica was in the house, that was where she put her purse. During their marriage, whenever they'd been out late at separate meetings, Jefferson immediately glanced at that sideboard on his return home to see if her purse was there. Telling him either that she was safely home or that he'd arrived first. In the latter case he'd usually pour himself a drink, go into the den and wait for her key in the lock.

Until tonight it had been a welcome sound.

"Why are you still here?" The question came just as he'd predicted. "Is everything okay? Kevin's not sick, is he?"

"Everything's fine."

He ached inside when she came over and sat on the floor at his feet, gazing up at him through the haze of lights. "What's wrong?"

Nothing. Everything. He'd divorced her to get rid of this feeling of failure. This constant ache of loss. And now, because they were divorced, he ached more than ever. Everything was crazy. Spinning out of control. Impossible to set right.

"You had a date." There was no accusation in his voice. Or in his heart.

"Sort of."

Jefferson took a sip of his scotch, then set the glass back on the leather coaster. It wasn't like her to be evasive with him.

She'd just told him she was going out for dinner. When she'd said she was going to the Prime Rib, he'd assumed it was a business meal.

"Kevin said you were with a man named Jack."

The pang that shot through him when she bowed

her head was almost more than he could bear. "I was."

"*The* Jack?"

"Yes."

"How long have you been seeing him?"

"I ran into him this afternoon when I took Kevin out for his picnic. It's the first I've seen or spoken to him since that week in New York."

Jefferson wasn't sure her answer made him feel any better. She'd just run into the man that afternoon and already they'd gone out. From her description of their time in New York, it had been the same way then.

Part of him was delighted for her. Relieved. Another part just plain hurt.

He looked down at her dark hair. "Is he living in the city now?" It was a comfort having her there with him, on the floor by him, where she'd sat so often over the years. They used to solve all the problems of the world this way, talking long into the night.

From the time he'd first known her, Erica had preferred to sit on the floor.

"He might be moving here." She answered him with only the slightest hesitation. Jefferson had no doubt that Erica would tell him anything he wanted to know. She'd always been honest with him.

"He's had an offer to head up a crisis-training center. They'd train not only for hostage situations but other types of crises, as well."

He was vaguely aware of the plans for this program. Government funds had been readily granted, the government wanted its citizens protected in all possible ways. Protected and prepared.

Jefferson had been unaware that Jack Shaw was involved. "Is he planning to accept the position?"

"He doesn't know yet." She shifted, hugged her knees to her chest.

"Do you want a drink? A glass of wine?" he asked before he remembered that this was no longer his house. He was playing host to her in her own home.

"No, thanks, I had a couple of glasses at dinner."

Since Kevin's birth, a glass or two of wine was the most she ever had. She'd said she wanted to be sober and capable at all times, because with children you never knew when an emergency might arise.

Jefferson had curtailed his drinking, as well. One a night was all he usually allowed himself.

"Did you tell him about Kevin?"

"Of course not!" A hand on his knee accompanied the words. Without any forethought, Jefferson covered her hand with his own and wasn't surprised when she leaned her cheek against his leg.

They sat quietly for several minutes. Jefferson watched the lights from outside, some blinking, some coming on, others going off, still others never changing. Why couldn't his relationship with Erica have been like those never-changing lights? They'd had a good life together. A relatively happy life until that fateful week in New York.

Or maybe only one of them had been happy....

Rising to her knees, she kissed his hand where it lay, still entwined with hers. She was so young. So beautiful. Where his skin was lined, his eyes surrounded by crow's feet, her features were perfect. Smooth. Pure.

"I gotta tell you, Jeff," she whispered, resting her head on his thigh. "I miss you so much."

"I miss you, too, honey." It was the first time he'd admitted as much to her, despite the wakeful nights he'd spent, longing for her presence.

Her head lifted; she leaned forward on his lap, her face almost level with his chin. "Why couldn't we have just been happy with what we had?" she said, her eyes clear even in the darkness. But her voice carried the pain she wouldn't let him see.

God, he'd never meant to hurt her. It was the one thing he'd promised himself he wouldn't do. And lately he couldn't seem to do anything else.

How could he love her so much, and yet feel so adamant about being through with their marriage? How could he love her so much and love Pamela, too?

"Because what we had wasn't enough," he told her. Was there no end to the pain? For any of them?

"Why?" Her voice revealed a hint of tears, but he knew she'd never let them fall. "Because of Pamela?"

"Partially." He had to be honest with her. "But more because of you, Erica. I know I'm not the right man for you."

"I'm old enough to make that decision."

"Maybe," he said. "But I'm discovering that age has nothing to do with one's ability to fool oneself. I know what a woman's supposed to feel when she sleeps with a man, honey, and you didn't feel it when you slept with me."

"Does Pamela?"

"She wants me, yes."

Erica slid back down to the floor, but she didn't let go of his hand.

"Kevin and I need you."

Not nearly as much as he needed them.

"Let me ask you this, Erica. When you were with that man tonight, did you think about going to bed with him?"

"Yes." Though he'd been fully prepared, the word cut into him.

"Because you wanted...Jack?" *The way Pamela wants me?*

She took too long to answer. Fighting a mixture of rage and despair, Jefferson sat there, holding her hand, swallowing back tears.

"Yes." He could have been forgiven for forgetting the question, so long had it taken her to answer.

But he hadn't forgotten.

Pamela should be at her condo soon. He'd rented

a place in her building. She'd be expecting his call. A call he very much wanted to make.

Which made no sense to him, considering how tempted he was to stay right here in the place he'd shared with his young wife for more than seven years.

"What we had was much more important than bed, Jeff," she said. "Love. Respect."

He noticed she left out a word she'd always included when she defined their relationship in the past. A crucial word. *Trust.*

She no longer trusted him. He'd betrayed her.

"And that didn't keep either one of us faithful to the other."

He hadn't meant to hit so low, but he was getting desperately close to begging her to give them another chance. He had the crazy feeling she'd go for it. But not because she was any more in love with him now than she'd ever been.

He was tempted to beg, anyway. And knew that doing so would be dead wrong.

She released his hand. Went back to hugging her knees. He'd won his battle.

It was the emptiest victory he'd ever known.

JACK CALLED Friday morning. Erica met him for dinner that night and the next couple of nights as well. They met at restaurants, nowhere private. Always after Kevin was tucked into bed and asleep for the night. They caught up on the past six years of their lives, observations they'd made, things they'd learned. It was as though they'd always known each other, from before time began. They shared an understanding that was uncanny.

There was so much to catch up on, so much to say, that day-to-day details were often forgotten or ignored. But that certainly didn't hinder their enjoyment of each other or the hours they spent together.

As in New York, before the final night, there was no sex. Other than that first night here in Washington, there wasn't even any kissing. Just tender touches now and then. Looks.

Maybe some unspoken desires.

It was a time out of time once again. An interlude. When Jack got a call, he'd be gone. Maybe never to return.

Sunday night Erica was smiling when she let herself into the condo. For the first time in months she had a bounce in her step, excitement in her heart. Jack was good for her.

Her smile faded when she saw Kevin sitting on one of the new chairs in the den, his little legs sticking straight out in front of him. He was fully dressed, slacks, shirt—buttoned crookedly—and his brown dress shoes. She'd left him in Power Ranger pajamas, sound asleep in his bed. The first thing that struck her was that he hadn't put on the tie. The second was the relieved look on the baby-sitter's face.

Katie, a cute blonde from downstairs, was in the

chair opposite him, leaning toward him as though they'd been in earnest conversation.

"What's going on?" Erica asked, keeping her voice light as her mind jumped ahead to possible crises.

Katie sat back. "I was in the other room watching TV when I thought I heard something. I came looking and he was just sitting here. I can't get him to talk to me, other than to say he's waiting for you."

Watching her son, who looked perfectly normal—if sitting up fully dressed, staring out a wall of windows after eleven o'clock at night, could be considered normal for a five-year-old—Erica forced herself to remain calm.

Approaching the chair, she knelt down, putting both arms across her son's lap. "Kevin?"

"Hi, Mom," he said. "I'm really tired. Can I go to bed now?"

"Of course," she said, picking him up to carry him back to his room. She nodded to Katie to let herself out, mouthing that she'd pay her in the morning. "Mind telling me why you got up to begin with?" she asked Kevin as they made their way down the hall to his room.

"I woke up."

"And you couldn't get back to sleep?"

He leaned back in her arms, playing with the Madonna-and-child charm on her necklace. "You weren't here."

"But Katie was."

"Yes, but she's not one of us, you know, who cares about our things."

Setting her son down on his unmade bed, Erica took off his shoes, dropping them on the floor. "She's one of us while she's here," Erica said. "She takes good care of you."

"But I'm the man now," he said sleepily, submitting without argument as Erica helped him out of his clothes and back into the pajamas she'd found in a heap on the floor.

That pair of little-kid pajamas was almost Erica's undoing. There were so few things that were still childish about her son.

"No, Kevin," she said, pulling the pajama bottoms up and settling them around his waist. "You're the little boy."

With a yawn, he lay back on his pillow and allowed her to tuck him in.

"You let Mommy take care of you for now, okay?"

He nodded. Gave her a hug so strong it hurt her neck.

Feeling a little better, if not completely without apprehension, Erica checked to make certain the Power Ranger night-light was on before flipping off Kevin's lamp. His eyes were already closed. With a long look back, she tiptoed to the door.

"It's okay, Mom." His sleepy voice stopped her in her tracks. "If you want to go out, I don't mind sitting in the chair till you get home, like Daddy used to do. It's not hard. I was just scared I might go to sleep...." His voice trailed off. In another few seconds, his breathing had grown slow and even.

Erica was thankful he'd fallen asleep so he couldn't know how badly his adult words—spoken in that childish voice—made her want to cry.

"YOU STILL SEEING Jack?" Jefferson was sitting in Erica's office. Having just come from a particularly grueling session with party leaders, he'd stopped by to fill her in on the stand he'd taken, and the possible damage control she'd need to do.

"He was called away on a job a couple of weeks ago." Two weeks and three days since she'd last seen him—the night she'd come home to find Kevin waiting up for her.

Jefferson's eyes narrowed. "So he didn't take the job here?"

"He hasn't decided yet."

"You've been in touch with him since he left?"

"He's called a couple of times." She wasn't sure what to make of that.

"Something he didn't do before," Jefferson noted. He was turned slightly sideways in the leather armchair in front of her desk, one knee crossed over the other.

"I know."

"Pretty significant, wouldn't you say?"

Looking at her ex-husband, the man she'd never

have divorced if he hadn't insisted on it, Erica wanted to scream.

"It's just a couple of phone calls, Jeff." That was what she'd been telling herself, too.

"You gave him your number." It was unlisted.

She shook her head. "He calls me here."

"Does he ever ask about Kevin?"

She frowned at him, trying not to feel defensive. "Why should he?"

"He hasn't?"

"No." But then, she'd purposely mentioned her son as little as possible.

"Maybe you should tell him."

"No." She hated this. Discussing the cause of the greatest pain she'd ever inflicted on anyone.

"Not now, of course," Jefferson said. "We can't risk it while Kevin's still so fragile. But eventually—"

"No. He's your son, Jeff. Let's leave it at that." She picked up her pen and pulled a legal-size yellow notepad toward her. "Now tell me exactly what happened this morning...."

Jefferson filled her in on the latest dispute over nuclear-weapons funding—a dispute that was growing more fervent, thanks to renewed fear of nuclear destruction. Jefferson opposed all funding for the rebuilding of nuclear weapons, and he was completely at odds with anyone who supported it. Not only would stockpiling these weapons heighten anxiety and intensify the threat of war, but nuclear storage facilities were far too damaging to the environment and to the people who lived near them. Long after they'd discussed strategies for presenting his view to the press, long after he'd left, their earlier conversation was ringing in Erica's ears.

Jefferson thought Jack's phone calls meant something.

And they couldn't.

ERICA WAS AT HER DESK, editing a speech Jefferson was due to give later that Thursday afternoon, when there was a tap on her door.

"Hi, Rudy." She smiled as she recognized the indefatigable reporter. "Come on in."

He was a small man who almost crackled with energy. He bounded into her office and into her leather chair.

"What can I do for you?" she asked, glad to see him. She and Rudy had developed a professional friendship over the past few years based on mutual respect and a shared distaste for Rudolf Valentino—Rudy's namesake.

Rudy was good at what he did. So was she. And somehow they managed to get their jobs done without stepping on each other's toes.

"You're not going to like it."

He didn't quite meet her eyes. A first for him.

"What garbage have you picked up out of the gutter this time?" Her voice was carefully nonchalant. All senses were on alert.

He shook his head, casually resting his chin on his knuckles, his bright gaze the only indication of his intensity. "I didn't get it off the streets, and this time, it's not garbage. I have proof."

Her stomach dropped. But not far. She knew Jefferson inside and out, and there was nothing for any reporter to find.

"Spill it, Rudy, so I can dispel whatever misinformation you've got and carry on with my day. It's a busy one."

"Kevin isn't Jefferson's son."

"Of course he is." Erica had no idea how she managed the words. Wasn't sure they even mattered. Rudy must have noticed how the blood had rushed from her face.

"Uh-uh." He shook his head again. "Jefferson Cooley's sterile. Mumps. His senior year in college. He missed a semester. Saw Dr. Hubert Langdon."

Mind scrambling, Erica did her best to look calm. To *feel* calm. Damage control. That was what she needed.

"I don't know where you're getting your information," she said as though it couldn't possibly be credible, "but more importantly, I don't know why. What in the world could you want with my husband's medical records?"

"Ex-husband."

"Ex-husband," Erica murmured. She thumbed through the papers on her desk, the speech Jeff was waiting for.

"So you don't deny it? Jefferson Cooley's sterile?"

"What possible reason could you have for asking such a thing?"

"Jefferson's topping the polls right now," Rudy said, any pretense of casualness gone. "Don't kid yourself into thinking Kevin's not part of the reason."

Erica didn't kid about things like that. She knew damn well what Rudy could do with such damaging information. But she wasn't yet sure how she was going to prevent him from using it.

"What do you want?" she asked.

"An exclusive on the real story about the breakup of your marriage. A sixty-five-year-old man doesn't leave a gorgeous young wife for a woman like Pamela Woods."

Men like Jeff did. Not that she expected Rudy, or indeed any of Washington's jaded contributions to humanity, to comprehend that.

She pinned Rudy with a hard stare. "I give you the inside scoop and you forget your doubts about my son's paternity."

Without blinking, he said, "Yes."

"I have your word on that?"

"Yes."

Studying him, Erica silently searched for any other solution. Over the years Rudy had established his trustworthiness. At least with her. Time and again he'd kept privileged information to himself; he'd also come to her on several occasions with threats to Jefferson's reputation and given her a fair shot at the other side of the story. She had no reason to doubt he'd do as he said.

It just meant that she'd have to swallow her pride in order to keep her world intact.

She thought of Jefferson. His career. The millions of people he affected. She thought of Jack. And she thought of Kevin.

"Okay."

"Hı."

Erica's heart leapt as she immediately recognized the voice on the other end of the line a couple of nights later. She'd only spoken to him on the phone twice in her life and already she knew his voice.

"Hi."

"How's your week been?"

"Busy. Good." If you didn't count the fact that she didn't dare leave her son with a sitter. That she had her hands full protecting her ex-husband's image. And that she was forced to see the half-truths she'd given Rudy—her claim that she hadn't been able to perform her "wifely duties" for Jefferson—smeared all over the local papers.

And some national ones, too.

"How about you? Where are you?"

Two weeks ago he'd called her from Texas. And last week from Kansas. Both times after being summoned by state police. One had been a false alarm—the person who said he had a little girl locked in a cabin with him had already killed the child, as the police discovered when they found her body in a gully. The other, a child-custody altercation resulting in a father holding his own son hostage, had had a successful conclusion. The boy had been returned to his mother. No one had been hurt.

"I'm home," he said now. "At my apartment in New York."

"The same one you had six years ago?" Not that she'd ever seen it.

"Yeah." There was a pause. "I picked up a copy of the *Times* today," he said.

The statement wasn't a casual one.

"You saw the article." It was inevitable. But still…

"I understand that your job is to make Jefferson Cooley look good," he said. She'd never heard this tone before. "I'm just not sure why protecting Jefferson means running yourself down."

She couldn't answer that. Not with the truth. "I don't always have a say in what reporters print," she prevaricated. And hated what the tangle of secrets and lies was doing to her life. They'd now infiltrated even the make-believe world where she and Jack lived.

She'd known that if they continued to keep in touch, it was bound to happen. But at the same time, she'd been trying to pretend that, as long he was nothing but an occasional long-distance phone call, she could keep him separate from the rest of her life.

It had been a stupid game to play. Of course he wasn't separate from her real life. He was the father of her child.

And every single day she had to bear the burden of knowing that when he didn't.

"You're asking for a retraction, then?" he asked after a moment, sounding somewhat mollified.

"No."

"Why not? Erica, you don't have to—"

"Jack," she interrupted. "It's not that big a deal. When you're married to a senator, you get used to seeing the occasional uncomplimentary article. I save my battles with the press for things that really matter."

She looked around the office she loved, the plants on the windowsill, the view overlooking Capitol Hill. Picking up a pencil, she tapped it against the pad in front of her. The one on which she'd just scribbled notes from her meeting with Jefferson. "Do you ever go to Maggie's?" she asked suddenly, not entirely sure why she wanted to know. It wasn't something she'd mentioned during their previous conversations. Neither had he.

"Occasionally."

"Just for a drink?"

"No." He paused and, dropping her pencil, she waited. "I go when I need to be reminded of certain feelings."

"Like what?"

"I'm not sure. Maybe the feelings that *don't* play a part in my life anymore."

"Then why do you want to be reminded?" she asked recklessly.

"For one thing it helps me in my work. The emotions responsible for some of the most heinous crimes are good feelings gone bad."

"Passion?"

"Yes."

Erica rested her forehead against her palm. A lack of passion had cost her her marriage.

But in another sense, it was passion that had brought the end of the marriage. Passion for Jack…

"What do you think makes that happen?" she asked him. "Good feelings going bad?"

"Life, I guess. Circumstances. The things that happen to people."

"Tragedy."

"Sure, or abuse. But I think sometimes the reason is a lot more innocuous than that. Like perceptions that change over time."

She thought of Jefferson. Their relationship had begun as a good thing and eventually become a source of deep unhappiness to him. *She* hadn't changed; neither had her feelings for him. His desire hadn't changed, nor his will. But with the passage of time, what had once been a joy had, in the end, cost Jefferson his self-respect.

"So how do you trust in a good emotion when it can so easily turn bad?"

"I don't."

It didn't seem to matter that she'd already determined this for herself. His confirmation was crushing.

"So you only remind yourself of these feelings in order to better relate to your suspects?" she asked numbly.

"Not entirely."

She waited, picked up the pencil again. He didn't elaborate.

"So why else?"

"Because for a lucky few, the good feelings—the honest and powerful emotions—sustain them through a lifetime. Every once in a while I feel a need to remember that.''

The admission warmed everything that had been hurt and frozen in Erica. It worried her, too. Was *she* what reminded him of happily ever after?

That seemed to be what he meant. But she couldn't be.

Sure, in some inexplicable way Jack made her feel alive. Hopeful. But only because he was safely ensconced in a memory—a make-believe week in New York.

She kept waiting for him to mention the Washington job...and was relieved when he didn't.

Washington was real life.

Washington was Kevin. And Jefferson.

But still, as she hung up the phone, she was already hoping he'd call again.

CHAPTER TEN

KEVIN WASN'T GOING to preschool today. He'd turned five now and preschool was for babies. Kevin was through with being a baby. He was a man now. And it was almost summer, anyway.

As he buttoned up his shirt, struggling to get the buttons through the holes, he told himself a story about a big boy who knew all the colors and numbers and other dumb stuff they taught in preschool. The boy didn't care that he wouldn't get to be captain on the team when they played ball, and he didn't really want to do the clay stuff and...

Before he could get any further with the story, it was time to tie his shoes. He knew he had to keep the bows even so when he wrapped one around the other, he didn't end up with a long string, instead of a circle. Then all he needed to do was the necktie. He tried his best. Since he was a man now, he'd borrowed the tie Daddy had left the last time he was over. No more already tied ones with the little plastic things. Daddy had shown him how to put it on.

He expected he'd have to argue with Mommy, but no matter what, he wasn't going to school. He had to go to her work with her. He had to find out about the nucl'ar war missiles Daddy was fighting about. People talked about new wars a lot, and since Kevin was a man now, he might have to be a soldier, too. The idea scared him. But he had to find out why his mom and dad were so worried. That meant he had to be like Daddy and know everything. Important stuff. Not like colors and numbers. He had to learn about nucl'ar weapons.

He couldn't do that at preschool.

"HI."

"Hi."

Their conversations always started out the same. Jack liked the familiarity.

"How's your week been?" It was almost two months since he'd seen her.

"Okay. Where are you?"

"Home. New York." He looked around the apartment. The furniture that had come with the place. The bare walls. Naked windows except for the blinds that had been there when he'd moved in. Other than books and magazines, his skiing and other recreational equipment, his computer, there was very little of him in evidence.

Not much to leave behind if he took the Washington job. This was not something he talked to Erica about. Not for the first time, he wondered what her home looked like. The curiosity to know had grown gradually into a yearning. When had that happened?

"Jack?"

"Yeah?" It was midmorning. The July sunshine gave the city below a clear sharp brightness. Nothing like the dark mystery it had been the night before, when he'd wanted to call Erica and had no way of reaching her.

"Why are we doing this?"

"What?"

"We've been talking to each other every week for two months. Why, Jack?"

"Because we like our conversations?"

"Is that all?"

"No." Although his instinct was to be evasive, he couldn't. Not with Erica. "We like each other, too."

He thought of the night they'd spent together in New York. He'd been thinking of that night periodically ever since it happened. Sometimes with incredible thankfulness, sometimes with great regret. But lately he'd been remembering their time together with a longing he could neither explain nor deny.

"Do you think it's wise that we continue?"

"What do you think?" It was a cop-out but the best he could do.

"I think we're very good for each other." She spoke slowly, thoughtfully.

He relaxed a little as he watched a woman down below leave the building across the street and get into a cab. Because the sun was so bright, she was more shadow and outline than person, lacking the substance of a human form. Kind of like Erica?

In some ways, she was that unreal, that distant from him. Yet in others... "How so?"

"We talk about things that matter. Make the world a little clearer for each other."

He nodded. "From the very beginning we've created an environment that allows us to be open-minded about each other's thoughts and opinions. That's rare in today's world." He'd only now realized they had that. It was important.

"Knowing you're out there makes me feel a little less lonely."

Loneliness was part of his life, yet he supposed there was something to what she said. Some reason he kept calling her. And thinking about calling her.

And then an awful thought occurred to him. Turning his back on the sunshine, Jack asked, "Do you want me to stop calling?"

"No."

"Good. Now that we've established that it's okay to talk, are you going to tell me what's bothering you?"

"Do you ever wonder what's going to happen if this gets to be more than two strangers talking?"

"Don't you think it's already way past that point?" The words came out automatically; he'd certainly never planned to say them.

He tried to picture Erica in her office, as though imagining her there made the question more manageable.

"Didn't it happen the first night we met?" he asked quietly.

Jack paced the hardwood floors of his apartment, thinking. He knew from experience how to deal with situations that were threatening to detonate.

"Yes."

Her answer panicked him. So he did what he'd been trained to do when a topic reached an explosion point. He backed away. For the time being.

"Is anything else bothering you?" he asked.

She paused again. "Nothing you want to hear about."

"I didn't know there was anything you'd have to say that I wouldn't want to hear."

"We never talk about Kevin."

"You never mention him," he said.

"I know. And you never ask about him."

"Not because I don't want to hear about him."

"You're sure?"

He hoped so. The boy was hers. Not his. "Of course."

"He's scaring me."

He'd been preparing himself to hear about naughtiness, time demands, maybe some school—no, wait, it was summer.

"Scaring you in what way?"

"My little man-child is living, breathing and sleeping nuclear weapons. It's all he talks about. Whenever he plays, it's with his soldiers. He comes to work with me and asks everyone what they think about nuclear missiles. Last night I looked in on him before I went to bed and he was wide awake. When I asked what he was doing, he said he was figuring out how to fight the bad guys so they wouldn't drop their nuclear bombs on us.''

Jack frowned. ''Does anybody ever play ball with the kid?''

''Jeff used to all the time. He still offers, but Kevin isn't interested. He either wants to play senator and White House—a new game he came up with at the beginning of the summer—or he climbs on Jeff's lap and asks him the same questions over and over. Will the good guys ever get rid of nuclear weapons or will they always be there.''

''Have you talked to anyone about it? A professional.''

''He's been seeing a counselor since the divorce, but so far, nothing's changed. He's always been an intense little boy. And far too smart for his own good. Jeff and I treated him more like an adult than a baby from an early age, talking to him as though he could understand what we were saying. Hindsight being twenty-twenty, I'm afraid that was our first mistake.''

Jack wondered if he and Melissa would have done the same with Courtney....

''What does the counselor say?''

''She says it's normal for kids his age to go through stages where they obsess about one thing or another. With some boys it's guns or superheroes. With Kevin it's nuclear weapons.''

"So she thinks it's a stage that'll pass?''

"Maybe.''

"What do *you* think?''

"I don't know.'' Her voice dropped. ''A couple of weeks before school ended, he refused to go anymore. I've been bringing him to work with me, thinking it would help make him feel more secure if we kept him close. Now I'm wondering if it's only making things worse, if placing him in this environment is hindering him from being a kid.''

Jack was completely out of his element. He saved kids. He didn't, under any circumstances, raise them. "What does his counselor say about that?'' He said the only thing he could think of.

"That it might be good to get him in some kind of play group, but that being here with Jeff and me might be good for him, too.'' She sighed. ''Not very helpful, huh?''

"Sounds like the whole damn thing's a crapshoot.''

"Yeah.''

"So I guess you just have to trust your instincts and do what you think is best.''

"Jack?''

"Yeah?''

"I can't have a relationship with you.''

A young girl, maybe seven or eight years old, came running up the sidewalk. Jack watched as she went from the corner to the building across the street. She climbed the steps and disappeared inside. She should never have been allowed on the streets of New York by herself.

"You want me to stop calling."

"No! I…just…I've… Twice I've been blindsided, you know? I go along, thinking life is fine, only to find out that I'm not seeing what the other person is…. I'm sorry, I'm not making any sense."

"Yeah, you are. Go on."

"When I'm in a relationship, I can't seem to tell if I'm making my partner happy. I've been through two broken marriages and I didn't have any idea that the breakup was coming in either case. I can't do that again. Can't go through worrying it might happen, constantly looking for signs or signals that I never seem to notice, anyway."

Jack was almost ashamed at the relief that flooded through him. "You've been hurt in a very private personal way."

"Yeah."

"Me, too."

"So we're okay, just to talk?"

He couldn't come up with any better alternative. "Yeah."

"Your calls help a lot."

They helped him, too.

JEFFERSON WAS TAKING some serious hits, Erica knew, with his support of the environmentalists who opposed funding for more nuclear weapon facilities across the United States. He didn't want his loved ones living by or working in any such facility; how could he support other Americans having to do so? Waste disposal alone was too big a risk factor.

That didn't even take into account the question of whether they weren't just asking for worldwide annihilation by considering a program to once again build weapons that could wipe out entire cities. He'd never believed that possessing nuclear weapons served as a deterrent. The more the United States built, the more other countries would build until, one day, some rogue state decided to exploit its power to the final limit. Or some friendly nation became an enemy. Once the first bomb was dropped, it would just be a matter of trading targets until there was nothing left.

Jefferson was passionate about his stand.

It was up to Erica to present that stand to his peers—and to the world. She wrote speeches. Spoke to the press. Approved releases. Counseled and convinced until she could hardly think of anything else.

Except Kevin.

Nuclear weapons might never be more than stored threats to the world. But they were slowly killing her.

Her phone rang.

"Hi."

"Hi." Fighting the familiar twist of desire at the sound of that voice, Erica looked out her office window and watched the people hurrying along the street. The sun was shining on the nation's capital.

"How are you?"

"Same as I was yesterday," she said, trying to contain the happiness she felt at hearing from him so soon. Since she'd told him about Kevin, he'd been calling a couple of times a week. "What's up?"

"I'm worried about you."

That made two of them. "I'm fine. Just tired."

"How's Kevin?" The question came as it always did since their conversation almost a month ago, with a mixture of compassion and reticence.

"More frenzied than I'd like."

"Has he got any new interests?"

"None." Ridiculous as it was, she found an odd comfort in sharing her worry about Kevin with his father. In this, it didn't seem to matter that neither boy nor man had any idea of their relationship.

She was trying to relax about that. She knew her decision to keep her secret was the right one for everyone concerned. And because her own relationship—for want of a better word—with Jack was a long-distance one, it was relatively easy to keep Kevin's paternity from him. Since his visit to Washington, he'd never mentioned the new job. She assumed he'd turned it down.

"So what's it going to take to get you feeling like yourself again?"

"The nuclear bill is coming up in another month. They're holding a special vote in early October. And

Kevin starts first grade. I'm relying on both of those things to make life a little less demanding.''

''He's in a private school, I hope.'' The immediate sharpness in Jack's voice was a bit of a shock. He was usually so calm.

''Of course.''

''It should be a small one. Security's easier to manage.''

''It is.''

''I'm assuming you've chosen one that's used to having senators' kids.''

''Yes.'' She frowned. Before now, Jack had just listened when she spoke about Kevin. Or asked her if she'd ''talked to his counselor.''

''They've got the means to provide proper protection?''

''Yes.''

''And it's close by?''

''Right down the street.''

''So you'll be taking him and picking him up.''

''Either I'll do it or Jefferson will.''

''Are there any provisions for concealed-weapon detection?''

Jack, who usually instilled a feeling of safety and peace, was starting to scare her. ''It's only first through third graders,'' she told him.

''Right,'' he said slowly after a brief pause. ''Sorry.'' His tone had changed.

''No problem.'' She was glad he cared.

''My beeper just went off. It's urgent.''

"Okay." She knew what that meant. It had happened before. "Be careful."

She could tell his mind had already left her as he muttered goodbye.

For the first time Erica wondered how much longer she could pretend that she didn't worry herself sick whenever he got a call.

Would this be the time he got shot?

And who would notify her if he did? Who—besides Jefferson—would know that Erica Cooley had even met a hostage negotiator named Jack Shaw?

"I'M WORRIED about you."

Erica looked up to see Jefferson standing in her doorway.

What was it with the men in her life? They all seemed to be worrying about her. It wasn't as if she hadn't survived every single crisis she'd ever had to face.

Of course, "men in her life" was a relative term. Men *outside* her life, on the periphery of her life, having once been in her life, but not now—that would be a more appropriate description. At the moment Kevin was the only man in her life. And she'd give just about anything to have him be a little boy again.

"There's nothing wrong with me that a good night's sleep and some exercise won't cure," she told him, smiling.

He came in and closed her door. Erica's smile faltered.

"What's wrong?"

"Nothing." He didn't meet her eyes. "I just wanted to discuss something with you that I'd rather not have overheard."

He sat in the chair in front of her desk, resting an elbow on the arm.

Alarm struck her. "What is it, Jeff? You aren't...sick or anything, are you?" It had always been a secret fear of hers. That he'd have a heart attack or develop some other critical illness. He drove himself as though he was thirty, rather than sixty-five. Sometimes she'd forgotten he wasn't closer to her own age.

"No, I'm fine," he assured her, looking up with a completely reassuring grin. "Just had my yearly physical this week, as a matter of fact. Not even a tinge of high blood pressure to worry about."

She relaxed, leaning back in her seat. "So what's up?"

"What do you think it would do to my image if I got married?"

Her heart froze. "Now?"

"I'm not sure." His eyes, when they finally met hers, were filled with compassion. Pain. Anticipation, too.

"You're thinking of asking Pamela to marry you?"

"Yes."

"Why?" It wasn't a proper question. She asked it, anyway.

"Because I love her."

Erica was honestly pleased to hear that. Relieved. Thankful that he had a chance to be happy.

Yet something inside her was dying. This was almost worse than when he'd asked for the divorce. This was the death of all hope. Not that she'd really expected them to get back together. She'd probably consider marrying Jefferson again if he'd asked…but she knew it would be for the wrong reasons. A desire for security, for protection from life's emotional ups and downs, did not make a good basis for marriage.

"I'm sorry." Jefferson's voice was low, almost expressionless.

She hadn't realized so much time had passed. "No!" She jumped up, came around to sit in the chair next to his. In the old days she'd have been on the floor at his feet. "Don't be sorry, Jeff! I'm happy for you."

"You know I'll never stop loving you," he said now. His look, when he met her eyes, was dead serious.

"If you mean that," she began, choosing her words carefully, speaking slowly.

"Of course I do," he inserted into the pause.

"Then do you think we should give us another try?" she asked.

Succumbing to her own needs, she dropped to the floor, her arms in his lap. "I can try to be different," she said, even while she knew in her heart that she wouldn't be. Had she been capable of feeling passion for Jeff, she'd have felt it long ago. But... "Think of Kevin..." she whispered.

His glance was warm, familiar. He was considering her request. Was going to say yes. Erica was flooded with relief. And joy, too, she supposed.

And then he shook his head.

"Why?" But she knew.

"Are you still talking to Jack every week?"

"Yes."

She knew the phone calls would never lead to anything else. That she couldn't allow them to. Because of Kevin, of course, but for her own sake and Jack's, as well.

But Jefferson realized that she'd never be able to respond to him with the passion he wanted. Needed. Deserved. Because for some reason, Jack was the only one who'd ever been able to excite that particular feeling within her. Under those circumstances, living with Jefferson would be unfair to him and their son. Her feelings for Jack—whether she chose to do anything about them or not—would damage all of them. They'd been through this.

"Do you...when you're with Pamela, does she...do you..." She didn't know how to ask if he was able to forget Erica when he was in the other woman's arms.

He seemed to understand exactly what she was

asking. His eyes were clear and bright as he looked down at her.

"Yes."

Erica felt like crying.

CHAPTER ELEVEN

RUDY STOPPED BY to see her again. He wanted to know how the senator planned to vote on an upcoming budget issue. It was information he knew Erica wouldn't give him. Except that he had an ace to play.

Pretending a calm she didn't feel, she bought herself a couple of days. But she was still shaking an hour later when she sought out Pamela Woods.

The tall, slender, gray-haired woman was standing at a bookcase in her office, reaching up for a book. Erica waited in the doorway for a moment, watching her from behind. With those long legs, the classic hairstyle, the deep-lavender silk business suit, she looked regal and every bit the successful attorney she was. Erica could see how Jefferson might fall for such a woman.

Still, it hurt.

"Oh!" Pamela said, turning. "Erica, I'm sorry, I didn't know you were there."

"I should have said something."

"No, no, that's okay. Come on in."

It was odd hearing that eager tone from a woman who usually spoke with such authority and confidence. This woman was the one person in the world who made Erica feel unsure of herself. Was it possible she had the same effect on Pamela?

It was something to ponder. Another time, perhaps.

Closing Pamela's door, she took a seat across from the other woman's imposing oak desk. There wasn't a paper or a folder out of place.

Erica's desk was usually littered with ten projects at once.

"What can I do for you?" Pamela asked. She sat in the chair beside Erica's rather than in her own behind the desk.

"I have a problem I need to discuss with someone...."

"Okay."

Reading the other woman's open gaze, Erica relaxed a little. "It's a rather sensitive issue."

"I figured as much, or you wouldn't be here."

She was smart, too. Of course, she wouldn't have held Jeff's interest if she wasn't.

Erica had to work hard not to let herself feel intimidated. "What I'm about to say is something that, in a way, I have no right to tell you, but I'm being subtly blackmailed."

Pamela sat up straighter. "Have you told Jefferson?"

"No." Erica shook her head and took a deep breath. "I know what he'll say if I do, but I also know it's not the best way to handle this. Problem is, I'm not sure what is."

Leaning toward Erica, both hands on the arms of her chair, Pamela said, "Why don't you tell me exactly what you're talking about and we'll see what we can figure out."

She'd come to the right place.

"Kevin isn't Jefferson's son."

Pamela's gaze wandered and then settled back on Erica. "I know."

"You do?" She felt ridiculous when she heard her own incredulity.

And hurt beyond anything she'd have expected. Jeff had told this woman his and Erica's most private secret. She felt betrayed all over again. Worse even than when she'd walked in on the two of them in Jeff's office the year before.

With compassion in her eyes, Pamela nodded. "I know that Jefferson is sterile. It came out when he was telling me about his college experience and the year he got so sick...."

"So you know about—"

"I don't know who Kevin's biological father is," Pamela said before Erica could give her any more information. "Jefferson felt terrible when he realized the implications of what he *had* told me and refused to say any more. For all I know, you were artificially inseminated."

Erica nodded. Not in affirmation, just acknowledgment of possibilities.

With that issue taken care of, she got straight to the point.

"Rudy Wallace found out about Jefferson's sterility."

"Oh, God."

"The first time he came to me with the information, he promised not to use it if I gave him a behind-the-scenes exclusive on my divorce. I made the mistake of believing him. He wrote the piece—and now he's back."

"The article that came out about a month ago, quoting you as admitting that you weren't able to, uh, perform your marital duties?"

"That's the one."

"Jefferson was pissed as hell about it."

"I know." She'd been on the receiving end of her ex-husband's temper for an hour over that. It had been an odd experience, having Jefferson fume at her.

"And now Rudy's pressuring you again," Pamela said.

"He wants to know where Jefferson stands on the budget."

"You can't tell him."

Erica looked at the woman and then said what they both had to be thinking. "But I can't let him print that story about Kevin."

"There's no other alternative. Jeff wouldn't want you withholding it for his sake."

Pamela's familiarity with Erica's ex-husband was hard to take. "I know."

"So let's consider what would happen if it came out."

Erica shook her head, adamant. "It can't."

"Why not?"

"Well, the most obvious reason is Jefferson," she said. "With his opposition to nuclear rebuilding—and people accusing him of being afraid to support a bold move—on top of the divorce, the bad press could kill him, and I've already hurt Jeff more than I can stand. I can't do it any more. Ever. If I can give him nothing else, he's got my loyalty for life."

"It's a good reason. Very good. But maybe not enough."

Humiliated by what she had to say next, Erica glanced down at the black pumps she was wearing. They were suede. Matched her black suede suit.

"If this gets out, Kevin's biological father will know that Kevin is his."

Pamela didn't flinch at the backhanded but still obvious admission of Erica's adultery.

"Shouldn't he know?" There was no condemnation in the older woman's voice.

"No," Erica said. And then, "I agree that a man deserves to know when he's fathered a child, but this is different. The news would be devastating to…this man." Briefly she told Pamela about Jack's past. "He won't risk losing so completely again. So he's avoided the commitment of family."

"But if he's faced with a fait accompli…"

"I don't think so," Erica said. She told Pamela a

little about Jack's job—not that he was a hostage negotiator, just a law-enforcement official who faced frequent danger.

"So, another good reason," Pamela conceded. "But still, maybe not enough."

"The strongest motivation is Kevin himself," Erica said, her confidence returning as she thought through the situation. "You spend time with him," she said, hating to acknowledge Pamela as a part-time mother figure in her son's life. "You know what a hard time he's having. There's no way I can upset him with a scandal like this."

"Even worse than the scandal is the shake-up it would bring to his entire world if he found out Jefferson wasn't his father. You and Jeff are the little guy's sole security, and that's already taken more of a beating than he seems able to handle at the moment."

Erica swallowed, impressed by Pamela's sensitivity. For a split second she experienced the bizarre impulse to lay her head on the other woman's lap and be comforted.

"So what do you suggest I do?" she asked.

"Let me talk to this reporter," Pamela said. "It's possible that a lawyer's perspective might change his mind. Blackmail's not only ugly, it's illegal."

"So he stops harassing me, but what's to stop him from printing the story?"

"He's already blackmailed you," Pamela said, smiling as though the two of them shared a secret.

"He prints the story and we press charges. He doesn't, and we agree to forget the whole thing."

"You're good," Erica said admiringly.

"It's why I'm sitting in this office."

Arming herself for her meeting with the wily reporter, Pamela asked for particulars, dates and times, all of which she wrote down. They discussed exactly what had occurred between him and Erica—as closely as Erica could remember.

They agreed that they wouldn't mention this meeting to Jeff.

And then they'd finished discussing the problem.

"Do you ever wonder what it would be like if Kevin and his father had a chance to know each other?" Pamela asked, filling the awkward silence.

As eager as she was to escape, Erica couldn't deny the urge to speak about the things that tore at her heart. She wouldn't have chosen her ex-husband's lover, but there was no one else. She'd separated herself from friends her own age after her first divorce, preferring long weekdays to facing their sympathy—and hearing about their love affairs. And the people she and Jefferson had socialized with had all been his friends—his age—not hers.

"I think about what it would've been like if I'd met him before anything else happened. Before we married other people. Before he suffered so much."

"You don't ever think about them meeting as things stand now?"

Erica shrugged. "Of course I do, but I just don't

think that's possible. It's all so messed up. So unfair. Yes, I'd love to have them know each other. Kevin's father was really athletic. It would be great if Kevin learned to ski or mountain climb. And I've occasionally thought that Kevin could really help…the man, too. He's so good with kids it's obvious he has a deep affinity with them.''

''Sounds to me like there might be more unresolved issues here than you think.''

''Uh-uh,'' Erica got to her feet. ''In a perfect world, maybe, but not in ours.''

''In a perfect world, there wouldn't be any issues.''

Pamela's sardonic remark followed Erica out into the afternoon sunshine.

''Hi.''

''Hi.''

''I didn't expect to find you there.'' It was after seven in Washington. Jack had just called out of a need to hear her voice, even if only on an answering machine.

''Jeff and Pamela have Kevin for the night. I'm using the opportunity to catch up on things here.''

Erica didn't often speak of her ex-husband's girlfriend. ''She's moved in with him, then?''

''No. She'll go home. Kevin sleeps in Jeff's room when he stays over there.''

''You sound down. And don't tell me you're just tired.''

"Jeff told me last week that he's going to ask Pamela to marry him."

Sitting in a motel room in South Dakota, Jack winced. "You know that has no reflection on you, right?"

"I know that I'm playing him up as a man who, when given the opportunity to parade around a young wife, chose love and a woman of his own age, instead. And it's more than the image, it's the truth. Jeff's values aren't shallow, and his constituents deserve to know that."

If Jack had been capable of falling in love, he might have done so in that moment. "That's pretty selfless of you," he murmured.

"I don't think so," she said softly. "I betrayed him. He'd done nothing but treat me with love and kindness. He cared for me, gave me everything I'd ever asked for, and I thanked him by...well, you know how I thanked him."

Yeah. He knew. And much as he hated what they'd done, what that night in New York had done to her, he couldn't regret the memory. And couldn't seem to keep himself from thinking about making another one...with her.

"So what's up? Are you as tired as you sound?"

"I am."

"Where are you?"

"South Dakota. There was an attempted imitation of the Oklahoma City bombing. An entire day care in a government building was being held hostage by this guy after his bombing failed. Apparently he'd been trying to get someone to listen to him for more than a year about a problem he'd had with city water out on his farm. This week his wife was diagnosed with cancer and he's certain the water she's been drinking is responsible.''

Sitting on the edge of his bed, Jack leaned forward, elbows on his knees, and rubbed his face. He'd just been through the most impossible fourteen hours of his career. He couldn't seem to shake them.

''So what happened?'' Erica's voice was more than just soft. It reached out to him, pulling him toward her as though she was there in the room, not half a country away.

''I almost lost one.''

An image flashed before his eyes in slow motion, as it had been doing for most of the past hour. The smoking gun. The little boy lifted off the ground with the force of the shot. Blood. In the air. On the wall behind him.

''What happened?''

''I talked for hours, but there was no reaching this man. He wasn't going to be talked down. We had his wife come. She couldn't make a difference, either. He was just too consumed by grief and panic at the thought of losing her, and driven by the rage of believing it could have been prevented if the parents of those children had done their jobs properly....''

''How many kids were there?''

"Fourteen. Or so I thought. That's what the report said."

"There were more?"

"One. A little boy. The teacher thought he'd been picked up already. Instead, he'd been hiding behind a trash can. The rest of the kids had all been herded to one end of the room. I found a way to get in, distracted the guy long enough to get between his gun and those kids. I didn't count on the little guy who ran out because he thought he was safe when he saw me...."

"Oh, God. I'm so sorry, Jack."

That voice. Her voice. It had an uncanny way of soothing him....

"The lunatic shot him," he said, his voice a careful monotone. "The bullet went straight through him. I don't think I'm ever going to forget the shock on that little guy's face."

And wondering if that was how Courtney had looked. As though, in her baby state of complete physical vulnerability and dependence, something so painful was utterly incomprehensible. Did the shocked expression change with age? Or had Melissa looked the same?

It wasn't as though he hadn't seen people shot before. After all, he'd worked in law enforcement for years. Most recently, he'd been there when James Talmadge had taken his own life. But Talmadge had known what was coming. He'd made a choice.

Yes, Jack had witnessed shootings, but he'd never

seen a bullet go clean through the center of a body. Exactly as had happened to his wife and baby girl.

"Did he die?" Erica's voice caught.

Her compassion was a comfort he hadn't expected—wasn't used to.

"No," he said, although he wasn't sure that was a good thing. "The bullet missed his heart by a couple of inches. But it shattered his spine. They can't tell anything this early, and there've been a lot of medical advances, but it looks as though he could be a quadriplegic for the rest of his life."

Silence. "You did everything you could," she whispered.

"I know." It was insane for him to think he could've known about that little boy. Hell, not even the kid's teacher knew. But to think Jack had been right there and...

"Is there anything I can do?" Erica's sweet voice dragged him back from the jaws of hell.

"Yeah," he said. "Talk to me for a while."

"Of course."

"And then give me your home number so I know I can reach you outside business hours..." She complied without hesitation, and he wrote it down on a page torn from the local phone book.

He fell asleep with the piece of paper clutched in his hand.

GO, BABY. JOIN IN. You love baseball.

Sitting with Jefferson behind a bush in the park,

Erica willed her son to drop the shroud of responsibility he'd drawn around himself and be a little boy again. Even if only for the duration of the two-hour birthday party he was attending for Bobbie Naylor, the son of a woman on Jefferson's staff. The little boy who used to be Kevin's best friend.

Kevin didn't really have time for friends anymore. He was too busy saving the world to bother with swing sets, T-ball or make-believe. At least, any time Erica or Jeff tried to cajole him into taking part in children's activities, he seemed to have more important things to do.

Like asking the same questions over and over and over again.

The only game he ever wanted to play was war, and his counselor had advised Erica and Jeff not to play that with him. She thought if they ignored the unwanted behavior, it would disappear.

Erica wasn't so sure.

Kevin was sitting on a picnic bench, his little feet, in the wing-tip shoes he'd insisted on wearing, swinging back and forth several inches above the ground. From her distant vantage point, it appeared that he was watching the baseball game being organized on the grass in front of him.

"He's not going to do it."

Positioned beside her on the ground, Jeff was watching just as intently. "Yes, he will."

Teams were chosen. The parents approached

Kevin. Said something. He shook his head. They tried twice more.

And then, before the first pitch was thrown, they called to him again from the makeshift field.

Kevin didn't budge.

Jeff rose. "I'm going over there."

"No," Erica said, placing a hand on his leg. "He'll just take the opportunity to ask you about your meeting yesterday. Dr. Miller said to throw him out there with people who can't pander to his obsession and see what happens."

They watched silently for several heartbreaking minutes.

"What he needs is a father young enough to get out there on the field—like Tim Naylor," Jefferson murmured. "Someone who has the energy and bone density to get down on the floor and roughhouse with him after a fourteen-hour day at the office."

"What he needs is you back home." Erica had promised herself she wouldn't do this.

She turned her head, met her ex-husband's gaze and could have bitten her tongue. She was not only hurting herself, she was hurting him.

"I answered the phone when I was over a couple of nights ago," Jefferson said. "The night you had dinner with the Terratruce people."

She nodded. Terratruce, a nationally powerful group of environmentalists. That dinner had been three days ago. Wednesday.

"It was Jack."

Erica's nerves stilled. "You didn't tell me he called."

"He said he'd call back."

He hadn't.

Crushing disappointment surged through her.

"You need to tell him about Kevin, Erica."

No. She'd worn a pair of off-white linen shorts in deference to the August heat and humidity, and the grass was making her thighs itch. She shifted. And then shifted again, her eye on Kevin, her nerves tuned to the man who sat just behind her, his legs pulled up, his forearms resting on his knees.

Jefferson was wearing shorts, too. Other than his gray hair and the lines fanning out around his eyes, he could have passed for one of the fathers on that ball field with the rambunctious five-year-olds.

Kevin sat on the bench watching. All alone. His white shirt and tie were so pathetically out of place with the denim shorts, T-shirts and running shoes the ten other boys were wearing.

"Look at him," she said, gesturing at their son. "*I can't* tell him you're not his dad. I can't confuse his life any further."

Or hers. Or Jefferson's, either. He was the one who'd been there for Kevin's birth. Who'd taken middle-of-the-night feedings, walked endless hours with him when he'd been writhing with the pain of teething. He was the one who supported, spent time with, taught and most important, loved her son. He was Kevin's father.

Kevin understood that better than any of them.

"Kevin doesn't have to know."

She glanced over her shoulder at Jeff. "You can't expect Jack to find out that he's a father and then have no relationship with his son."

"Isn't that exactly what you think Jack would want?"

Shifting again, Erica turned. She couldn't bear to watch her son sitting there all by himself anymore. "It is what Jack would want," she said, "but it isn't what he'd do. In some ways he's a lot like you are." In a lot of ways. "He's responsible above and beyond his own self-interest. Plain and simple, if he knew about Kevin, he'd insist on being an active participant."

Frowning, Jefferson said, "Even if it meant harming him?"

"Of course not. But don't you see, there's no point in telling him. It'll only force him to do something that would be incredibly painful for him. It'll hurt you. And because Kevin isn't going to know, it won't make any difference to him, anyway."

Jefferson picked a blade of grass, looking down at the tennis shoes he was wearing without socks. "Are you so sure that knowing about his son would be painful to him?"

"Positive." Erica thought about the conversation more than a week ago when he'd told her about the boy in South Dakota. As they'd talked that night, he'd mentioned Courtney and Melissa more times than in all their other conversations combined.

"I told him about Kevin starting school," she said, repeating some of what she'd told Pamela. "He hardly knows Kevin, and he was almost beside himself with protectiveness, going way overboard, or saying that I should, to make certain he's safe." She smiled sadly up at Jefferson. "And that was only about going to school. Can you imagine what he'd put himself through enduring everything else a child experiences growing up?"

Maybe she'd been hoping Jefferson would have a different take on the situation or some insight she'd missed. When he remained silent, she was instantly depressed.

She told him about the incident last week in South Dakota, about Jack's inability to stop feeling responsible for something that was entirely out of his control.

"And aside from that, how could he possibly do his job, how could he walk in front of that bullet, if he knew he had a son of his own waiting for him, depending on him, back home?"

"Maybe he couldn't," Jefferson said, his face serious as he watched the ball game in the distance. "Of course, all hostage negotiators aren't single and childless."

"They aren't all like Jack, either."

They sat there for another hour, watching their

small son fight a battle he didn't need to fight, taking comfort from each other and sharing their pain.

The boys at the birthday party finished playing baseball. While the parents cut the cake and dished up ice cream, the boys played tag. They whooped and hollered and grabbed things the entire time Bobbie was opening his presents. They climbed on every available surface, including each other. They laughed.

Kevin sat alone at the picnic table.

THURSDAY NIGHT of the last week of August, Erica was already in bed when the phone rang. Putting down the novel she'd been reading—a comedy about a woman's attempt to make a movie in a small, closed minded town—she picked up the receiver.

"Hi."

She'd been hoping...

"Hi." Sliding down in the bed until her head lay against the stack of pillows she'd been using as a backrest, she welcomed the surge of energy Jack brought to her life.

"How are you?"

"Good," she said. The questions always started out the same. She loved being able to count on that.

Count on him.

"And you?" Her bare legs moved slowly, sensuously against silk sheets. "Where are you?"

"Just got home tonight. I've been in Quantico, giving a series of lectures at the FBI Academy."

"Did you enjoy it?"

"Yeah. It was great to be reminded of how I felt twenty years ago when I was just starting out, to get back to basics."

She wondered about the Washington job. But didn't ask.

"So, what have you been up to this week?" he asked. He sounded relaxed, unrushed, as if he had all night to chat.

Well, so did she. Until six o'clock the next morning, when she had to get in the shower.

"The usual," she said. "Things are really getting busy at work with the nuclear vote coming up in a couple of weeks. And I've been trying to get Kev ready for school. He's not interested at all."

At least she hadn't heard from Rudy again since her meeting with Pamela and the lawyer's ensuing session with the aggressive reporter. Not that that stopped her from worrying. Knowing he had the information was like sitting around waiting for a bomb to go off.

Then, too, if Rudy could find it, so could someone else.

"Things still the same with Kevin's obsessions?"

"Yep." She told him about the birthday party, but for some reason didn't mention the couple of hours she'd spent with Jefferson watching the whole sorry afternoon unfold.

They talked about his week and hers, some people she'd met, a particularly good meal he'd had, a joke she'd heard. About things in the news. And about a homeless man who'd been hanging around Jack's apartment building and the money he'd given him. He held the phone up to his CD player and had her listen to a cut from a new CD he'd purchased.

His voice expressed an entire range of emotions. From lazy to energized, lethargic to passionate.

Physically restless, in spite of how much she was enjoying the conversation, Erica moved all over her bed. She kicked off the covers. Lay on her stomach, propped up on her elbows, her feet in the air behind her. Then she sat up, hugging a pillow to her chest. She dangled her feet over the side of her bed. And pulled the covers up to her shoulders when she got chilled.

The silk pajama top that was the extent of her attire, other than a pair of very brief panties, rode up to her ribs, then fell to her thighs.

"You've mentioned all your obligations," Jack told her more than an hour into the conversation while she was playing with the silk-wrapped buttons that ran down the front of her shirt. "What about free time?"

She thought for a moment. "I guess there isn't any."

"In the months we've been talking, you've never mentioned a date."

Her fingers stopped moving. "There hasn't been one."

Was he dating? Was that what he was trying to

tell her? It was fine with her if he saw other women. Really, she expected him to.

Still…

"Why not?" His voice was low, husky.

Sexy.

"I'm too busy."

"That's weak."

"I don't want to leave Kevin with a sitter."

"You have Jefferson to watch him."

Lifting her hips, she pulled her shirt down, ignoring the wave of chills that swept over her as the silk slid along her stomach. She wrapped her arms around herself.

"What's the point of dating?" she asked as bluntly as she dared.

"Companionship?" It sounded as though he wasn't sure about that himself.

Studying the paintings of French street scenes aligned on one of her bedroom walls, she considered his suggestion. "I have all the companionship I need at the office with my co-workers. With Jefferson." She tried to leave it at that, but something pushed her to be completely honest. "And with you."

He didn't say anything for so long she started to feel afraid. Had she upset him? Their relationship was so odd there wasn't a single social rule to govern it. And they'd never established any of their own.

It was almost as if they didn't need them.

Or did they?

"What about sex?"

She felt desire, intense and unbanked. "What about it?"

"I would think you'd want it."

Toes curling, Erica slid down in the bed, her shirt riding up again. He had no idea....

"Contrary to my actions in New York, I can't have...sex without commitment. And that's a road I'm all done traveling."

"You can't know that." His voice wasn't quite so soft. "You're not even forty years old!"

"I'm old enough to have believed in 'till death do us part'—twice. And both times, I was powerless to cash in on any promises made to me when my partner changed his mind. 'But you promised' didn't seem to mean a thing."

"Not all men are unfaithful."

"No, but all people make promises they don't keep."

"That's harsh."

She supposed it was. She suddenly felt so weary. And far too lonely.

"I might have a solution to your problem." His voice, a half whisper, slid over her, through her.

"What problem?"

"The sex one."

She'd just told him she didn't have a problem. "What's your solution?" she asked, anyway. Curious.

"Seems to me we're both in the same boat," he said easily. "Neither of us takes sex lightly, and yet neither of us is open to the possibility of commitment.''

That about summed it up. But if he thought having someone to share her misery was a solution, he was wrong.

She already had her solution. *Ignore the problem.* She had enough real problems to deal with.

''So?'' she finally said when it became obvious that he was waiting for her response.

''So, the solution seems obvious. We have sex with each other.''

She almost dropped the phone. *''What?''*

''It's not like we haven't done it before.''

Well, yes, but...

Damn her body for burning up at the mere thought.

''Like I said, it's the perfect solution. The parameters are set. We both benefit. What can it hurt?''

Her. The last time—the only time—she'd made love with him had changed her life irrevocably.

But then, Jack had no idea what kind of repercussions had resulted from that one night together. No idea that the child he assumed was Jefferson Cooley's was actually his own flesh and blood. He had no way of knowing that every time she looked at Kevin, really looked, she saw the man to whom she'd given her soul during one lost week in New York City.

''If we do that—'' she stopped. Licked her lips. She couldn't believe she was even having this conversation. But her body was remembering another time, and the liquid heat coursing through her belly was stronger than her sense of survival.

At least at the moment.

"If we do that," she started again, "don't we run the risk of getting too involved? I mean, how do you have such an…intimate relationship and stay emotionally detached?"

His silence made her uncomfortable. "*Are* we emotionally detached?"

"Isn't that what we're all about? No commitment? No risk?"

"Do you feel emotionally detached?"

The pain she heard in his voice forced the truth from her. "No." And then, when he said nothing, she asked, "Do you?" She held her breath—waiting for his answer—until she began to feel dizzy.

"No."

"So what does that mean?"

"Maybe it's not the emotional detachment that's so important."

Sliding down so that her head was resting on the pillows, Erica threw an arm across her eyes. "What else could it be?"

"Expectation." He said the word as if he'd only just discovered it. "If we have no expectation of each other, if we count on nothing, then we can't be hurt if we discover that nothing is all there is."

Sounded like a sell job to her.

It was a testimony to how pathetic she'd grown that she bought into it, anyway.

"So, if you're ever in Washington or I'm in New York, we have sex?" Desire curled through parts of her that had been ignored a long time.

"I'm willing to give it a try if you are." There was a funny lilt to his voice.

"Okay."

"Okay."

As she hung up and rolled over, turning off the light, her body, at least, hoped that he was going to be in Washington very, very soon.

CHAPTER TWELVE

MOMMY AND DADDY wanted him to go to school. That scared Kevin. How could he be ready to fight if he was locked away in a dumb classroom all day with a lady talking to him about apples and numbers and other junk that didn't have anything to do with nucl'ar munitions? If he wasn't at work, how would he ever keep up on things?

Daddy was trying hard to make nucl'ar munitions stay away, but he wasn't done yet. And some other big men were trying to stop him. Kevin heard him and Mommy talking in Mommy's office when he was supposed to be helping put papers in the shredding machine. He'd sat outside the door and listened, instead, until Bobbie's mommy came by and took him down to the candy machine and bought him his favorite chocolate bar.

That was nice. Maybe the best part about going to work.

Still, what could he do about school?

Daddy and Mommy had talked about the people who agreed with Daddy and wanted to help him. Mr. Terratruce and his friends. They were going to be having a rally soon. Rallies, Mommy had told him, were a lot like parties.

So, maybe he'd go to Mr. Terratruce's party. They'd probably talk about nucl'ar munitions there. Maybe they could even tell him how to know when he should be ready to fight.

Somehow he'd have to find out when Mr. Terratruce was having his party. And somehow he'd figure out how to get there. Mommy walked a lot of places. And Kevin knew his way around Capitol Hill. Maybe the party would be near the office, and he could just take himself.

Then Mommy and Daddy wouldn't have to know. They kept telling him not to worry about the missiles and munitions. They thought he didn't know about men having to fight. They acted like they didn't know he had to be a man now.

But that was okay. If they were scared like him and had to pretend, he could understand that. He did everything just like Daddy. He tied his own shoes and was pretty good at knotting a tie. He could go to the party and figure it all out, and Mommy and Daddy wouldn't have to be sad anymore.

"Hi."

"Hi."

There was no reason for Jack to feel so edgy. He'd been thinking about this phone call all day. Anticipating it. Looking forward to making it.

"How are you?"

"Okay." She sounded as weary as ever. Still, since their late-night call a couple of weeks ago, there'd been a certain indefinable something in her voice. Something that echoed deeply inside him.

"How about you? Where are you?"

"Washington." He stared out the window at the darkened street below, wondering how far away he was. Couldn't be too far. She'd said she was only a couple of blocks from the Prime Rib.

And so was he.

"You're in *town?*" Erica shrieked. He had to pull the phone away from his ear.

"Yes."

"Where? When? How long have you been here?"

Smiling, receiving an even more gratifying reception than he'd imagined, Jack sank to the floor of the still-empty apartment.

"I just flew in today," he said. And what a day it had been. He was exhausted, but feeling better than he had in a long time.

There were many things he refused to think about, but wasn't that how most people coped with life?

"How long are you in town? When can I see you?" His body was instantly hard as he recalled what they'd promised each other.

He'd been living with constant anticipation for weeks.

It was past ten. He'd purposely waited until he could be sure her son was asleep and her obligations pretty well through for the night. He wondered if she was in bed.

"Other than a trip back to New York to get a few boxes of stuff, I'm here permanently," he told her, looking around the first new apartment he'd had since Melissa died. The first home he'd ever had outside New York City.

All he could see was the bare floor and walls of the living room, but he'd been through the place thoroughly that afternoon and was pleased.

"You took the job?" she asked. Her voice, though lower now, was still excited.

"Yeah. It was time." He still couldn't get that little boy in the day care out of his mind. He'd had a call from the boy's parents. It appeared that with months of therapy the boy might become whole and well again. And still he haunted Jack.

"So where are you staying?"

"I've got an apartment on K Street. Just past Twenty-first."

"That's just around the corner from me!"

"I hoped it was." Yeah, it might be pitch-black in his living room—there were no overhead lights and he didn't own a single piece of household furnishing—but things were definitely looking better than they had in a long time.

In at least five years...

"When can I see you?"

"Tomorrow?"

"What time?"

If he'd been at all worried about her willingness to continue this crazy…whatever it was they shared, well, he needn't have bothered.

And at the moment, he was choosing to ignore any worries about the dangers of embarking on a relationship that wasn't part-time and wasn't long-distance. Neither of them had any expectations. That was what mattered.

"Any time that's good for you," he told her, wondering how long he'd been wearing the stupid grin on his face. "I've got a couple of days to get settled before I report for duty. Other than a quick trip back to Manhattan, I'm going to be spending my time buying furniture." He looked around. "And a lamp."

"I know some great places to get furniture."

He'd hoped she might. "You want to come along?"

"It'd be best if I got a look at your place first…."

"Meet me here tomorrow night at eight-thirty?" He knew she had dinner and a story with her son before that. The boy's bedtime was eight.

"Okay. As long as Jefferson's free."

Jack was still smiling when they rang off. He wasn't going to let a little twinge of something close to jealousy at the mention of her ex-husband mar what had been as close to a perfect day as his life could produce.

JEFFERSON WATCHED Erica get ready for her date. So now, in addition to every other sorry thing he'd learned about himself over the years, he'd discovered he was a masochist, too. He'd come early so Kevin could see him before he went to bed, to know that his father was there so he could sleep.

"Where are you going?" he asked as Erica came hurrying out of the bedroom he used to share with her.

He'd been living with a knife in his gut for more years than he wanted to think about. It twisted a little more sharply than usual when she wouldn't meet his eyes.

"I don't know. Dinner, probably."

"He's picking you up, then?" He was finally going to see the man who'd fathered *his* son—the son he'd never have had without Jack.

More masochism? Or maybe realism. Maybe he just needed to see the man, to approve of him, before he could finally let Erica go.

"No, I'm meeting him." She'd taken a lipstick from her purse, was using the mirror by the entryway as she applied it.

Dressed in black cotton stretch pants and a three-quarter-sleeve beige and black cashmere sweater, his communications director looked more beautiful than he'd ever seen her.

"If you don't know where you're going, how will you be able to meet him?"

She turned toward him, and for the first time, Jefferson saw the various emotions flickering in and out of her eyes. Excitement. Apprehension. A flicker he'd never seen there before. And, when she looked at him, unadulterated pain.

"I'm going to his new apartment."

The statement fell baldly into a room grown silent. Jefferson stared at her for as long as he could maintain his composure, and then he turned, facing the wall of windows that had been his salvation on so many occasions throughout the years of his life with her.

"He took the job," he said when he could.

"Yesterday. Yes."

"When are you going to tell him about Kevin?" He braced himself for the final fracture of everything he'd held dear for so long. He wouldn't just be losing Erica, he'd be losing his son, too. If not now, then eventually.

He'd resigned himself to never having children, and he'd been at peace with the situation. But that was before he'd had Kevin, before he'd known what it was like to have a son. To listen to those never-ending questions, feel the trusting, innocent touch of those small hands, watch the determination as life unfolded each new challenge.

"I'm not going to tell him."

"You can't have him here in town, part of your life, seeing the boy and not—"

He didn't know she'd moved until she was standing in front of him. She took both of his arms, her grip surprisingly firm, and looked up at him. "All the reasons we've already discussed still stand, whether Jack's in town or not,'' she said quite clearly. ''I love you, Jeff. There is no way on this earth I could take your son from you. Or you from Kevin.''

''Maybe you shouldn't go out with him. Maybe you're just asking for trouble.''

''You'd rather I lived the rest of my life alone?''

''No!'' Of course he didn't. ''Maybe I should move back in here, after all.''

What was he saying? Had he lost his mind? Was the thought of losing Kevin driving him over the edge?

She walked to the window, stood gazing at the lights glittering out in the darkness. ''Tell me something, Jeff.'' Her voice was cold.

He'd spent his entire life thinking of others, trying to do what was right. Only once had he dared to reach out for something for him, to believe that he could have it all. Did it really have to come to this?

''Anything.'' It was a physical pain to restrain himself from going to her, pulling her into his arms, hiding her away from all that hurt her.

''When you go into work tomorrow, when you see Pamela, could you in good conscience tell her you were moving back in with me?''

Pamela. Just the thought of her lightened some of the tension strangling his heart.

Erica had him there.

"I thought not." She turned, picked up her purse, went to the door.

"I won't be late," she said over her shoulder.

"Be as late as you need." He wasn't sure she even heard the words.

The door had already clicked quietly shut behind her.

IT WAS INEVITABLE that the moment Jack opened his door to her, Erica would fall into his arms. There simply was no other choice.

With his lips on hers he pulled her inside and kicked the door closed.

"Hi," he said when they finally broke apart.

"Hi." She couldn't stop smiling. He looked so good to her. Felt so good. It had been a long couple of months. Talking to him. Not seeing him. Longer, maybe, than the six years she'd lived without him.

"How are you?"

"Getting better by the second."

He was still holding her, his eyes on fire as they held her gaze. "I like that."

"Me, too." To actually be with someone you cared about and feel completely good for a moment—she could barely comprehend it, barely believe it.

He bent down to kiss her a second time, and Erica met his lips, freely giving him the passion she'd given with so much guilt six years before.

She was desperate to lose herself in Jack. To forget, just for a little while, the tangle of love and pain she'd caused. To be completely consumed by emotions, with no means of escape. No alternative but to hang on and ride.

"What you do to me, woman," Jack whispered hoarsely. He nudged her, kissing her again, until she was pressed against the wall. Erica eagerly accepted the extra support, spreading her legs enough for him to fit between them.

Jack's lips clung to hers, his tongue approaching hers boldly. Shaking with the intensity of the passion he aroused in her, Erica was just as forward, with her mouth, her tongue, her hands. Intoxicated by freedom, she touched Jack everywhere, needing all of him at once.

There were too many years to make up for. Too many regrets.

Fear spurred her on, too. Was this all a dream? Something that would fade away into darkness?

Jack lifted his mouth from hers, his lips trailing wet and hot down her neck. "I'm sorry," he said raggedly just beneath her ear.

"Don't be." She was well beyond being embarrassed by the moan that accompanied her words.

His hands beneath her sweater were such a long-awaited relief she almost cried. She laughed, instead, a sexy release of glad anticipation she didn't even recognize.

"You like that?" Jack murmured, his lips against

hers again. His thumbs teased her nipples through the thin spandex of her bra.

"Oh, yeah." Erica arched involuntarily, her hips bumping his, sweet feminine need against hard solid male. Rubbing herself against him, she groaned. She'd had no idea life could be so unbelievably fine. Had never, even during their night together in New York, been as alive, as wholly invigorated, as she was at that moment.

She wanted to touch every part of him, to experience everything she'd fantasized about, all the things she'd agonized over never having the chance to do. But as Jack's hands slipped inside her slacks, she just held on. First with her arms wrapped around his back as his fingers cupped her bare bottom, and then, when he slid her pants down to her ankles, her hands moved up to clutch shoulders suddenly naked.

There was no time for thought, or finesse. No time for pretty words—or any words at all. One second they were two sane responsible adults and the next a couple of starved needy lovers, grasping. Gasping. Making something out of the nothing they'd had for so long.

As soon as their clothes were scattered heaps on the floor, Jack was kissing her again, never ceasing his onslaught on her senses as he sheathed himself in a condom that seemed to appear from nowhere. He lifted her easily, holding her up as he found her center, and then he slid her back down against the wall and entered her. Legs wrapped around him, Erica held on to those magnificent shoulders and shuddered with the force of the convulsions spreading through her.

He didn't falter. Didn't stop. Just continued to hold her against him and thrust that powerful body into hers—making her his and making him hers in the most elemental way.

No matter what else was wrong in their lives, in her life or his, this sublime joining felt ordained. Completely right. Something beyond the normal realm of their experiences.

She and Jack. Together. A piece of heaven.

CHAPTER THIRTEEN

"WHAT'S WRONG?"

Erica didn't know how to answer the question. Jack had been in town a week, and it had been the best week she'd had since the first one she'd spent with him. They'd had fun. Buying furniture. Talking over dinner without the dagger of time hanging over their heads. Having no fear of saying goodbye, because it wasn't forever.

Making love. That part of her life was unbelievable.

In the dark, sitting on a park bench halfway between his home and hers, she wished they hadn't decided to take this walk. That they'd said their goodbyes at the restaurant and she was home in the privacy of her bedroom, where no one knew what she did or thought.

Home with her son—their son—sleeping across the hall.

She didn't know how much longer she could be with Jack, spending incredibly intimate moments with him, and not tell him that he had a son. The omission was growing into a barrier between them. One she couldn't break down. Or climb over.

"I don't know," she said when the silence was becoming more uncomfortable than the truth. "Why does anything have to be wrong?" It was a stalling tactic, both an honest query and a plea.

"We've seen each other four times this week. You've become more reticent each time."

"Maybe just knowing there'll be other days to discuss things, I don't feel the push to do everything at once."

She hoped he'd accept the explanation.

And that he wouldn't.

On the surface, things were perfect between them. They had it all. Each other and freedom. Companionship and no risk.

She didn't think she could go on much longer.

His shoulder touching hers, he turned and looked at her beneath the September moonlight shining through the trees. Another time she would've welcomed the opportunity to see inside him. Tonight she looked away.

"It's not the conversation," he said. "It's this." He gestured between them. "There's something missing. Or am I imagining things?"

"You aren't imagining anything."

"I didn't think so."

"Is it just me who's having problems?" she asked.

He shook his head.

Tears burned the back of her throat, although she wouldn't let them fall. "What's the matter with us?"

"Maybe it's the proximity. What we had was

so…close because there was always a clock ticking. You want what you can't have.''

"Do you believe that?''

"No.''

"So what is it?''

"I honestly don't know.'' He shook his head. Held her hand. "I can't think sometimes for wanting you.''

Erica had never been a woman to heat up easily, so she was still a bit shocked at how readily he could arouse her. Just that one sentence and she was on fire. "Me, too.''

"Tell me what you're feeling.''

Erica shrugged, taking comfort from the touch of their shoulders. "I love being with you,'' she said, delving deep inside. "You make me feel better than I've ever felt before. Life is exciting and full of promise I didn't even know existed.''

"And that's a problem?''

"No.'' She grinned at him, but sobered quickly. "I can't wait to be with you. And as soon as we're apart, I'm looking forward to the next time.''

"And *that's* the problem.'' It wasn't a question now.

"Maybe.'' There was so much swirling around inside her. A need to share her son with his father. A stronger need to protect all three of the men in her life. From her mistakes. From each other.

The need to be free from the kind of risk that

caring about Jack imposed—the risk of losing everything all over again.

"When does enjoyment turn to need? And isn't need just another word for expectation?"

"I don't know." He sighed. These thoughts were obviously not new to him.

"I'm afraid I'm going to screw this up for us, break our rules," she said.

She was scared to death that he was going to find out about Kevin—and that he wasn't. How could she be so close to him and yet conceal the most important thing they shared?

He wasn't saying anything.

Enduring the silence as long as she could, she finally said, "I'm not sure where that leaves us."

Lost. That's where. Right where she'd been since Jefferson had moved out. Or more likely, where she'd been since that week in New York when she'd fallen in love, conceived her son and ruined lives.

"We could go back to only talking on the phone." Had she been a better person, would she have offered to sever *all* contact? Wouldn't that be kinder?

"Is that what you want?" he asked.

She thought of Kevin. Of Jefferson. Wondering where love and loyalty would have her go.

"No." Because of the secret she had to keep, she had to be completely honest in everything else. Jack deserved that. So did she.

"I'm glad to hear that."

The intensity of her relief made no more sense

than the rest of her tangled feelings for this man. How could she need to run—and to stay—at the same time?

"We could limit ourselves to only seeing each other once a week, meet for dinner or something."

"I don't want to do that," he said.

Neither did she.

"We can make a vow not to have any more sex."

"I can't, can you?"

She looked at him, the broad shoulders, wind-blown hair, the fire burning in those eyes. And thought of the night before, when he'd held her so tenderly. "No."

He nodded, stood, held out a hand to her. "Let's walk."

Tension buzzing, Erica got up, eager to have something to do besides sit there and feel control of her life slipping completely away. They set out at a brisk pace, walking mostly residential sidewalks, not all of them lit by streetlights.

"Do you have a solution?" She'd been almost afraid to ask.

"No."

There was something else they weren't talking about. *Someone* else. She wasn't talking because there was so much she couldn't say. But equal significance lay in the fact that he wasn't talking, either.

And that she was thankful for his silence.

"I have a son." She'd meant the words to be uttered softly, not come blurting out like some sort of challenge.

"I hadn't forgotten."

"He's a huge part of my life."

"I know that, too." He took her arm as they veered around a missing piece of cement, and then kept her hand in his as they continued to walk. They'd slowed their pace.

"How can you be part of my life and not be part of his?" Her heart pounded as she traveled into territory too dangerous to navigate without damage.

She didn't know what she was looking for—reassurance that they could pull this off, or some small hope that he'd be able to handle a closer association with Kevin someday?

"I don't know." The words seemed to be torn from him. "But I do know that every time you talk about him I have to distance myself."

So much for hope. "Why?"

"Because if I don't, I'm going to drive us both crazy looking for all the ways he could possibly get hurt and then attempting to protect him."

"Maybe not if you're aware of that tendency."

"What I'm profoundly aware of, more so than most people, is how much danger lurks around every corner. Add to that a very personal awareness of the fact that it doesn't just happen to other people, and you have a man who borders on paranoid when it comes to children."

She thought of his reaction when she'd mentioned that Kevin was going to start first grade.

"You lost Melissa, too," she said. "Your wife. You tried to protect her. Why don't you feel just as strong a need to protect me?"

JACK'S HEART missed a beat at Erica's question. He was silent for a long time.

"I guess because we don't have a commitment," he finally said, knowing the answer was insufficient. "I don't have the right to tell you what to do."

"Doesn't caring for someone give you that right?"

He didn't want to talk about caring, either. Or where it could lead.

What he wanted to do was walk away fast. So fast he'd be running. The night air was making him claustrophobic—something he'd been feeling a lot recently. A condition he thought he'd beaten a few years ago.

What he wanted was to lose himself in her arms and never be found again.

"You're an adult. You're able to take care of yourself, which makes you much less vulnerable."

His argument was weak. And, he was fairly certain, completely invalid, as well. He just knew that he couldn't think about losing Melissa and continue to see Erica. And he couldn't stop seeing Erica.

Somehow, through some convoluted kind of logic,

he'd figured that if he could at least stay away from the kid, he'd be okay.

For the moment he was just grateful that Erica had accepted his feeble attempt at an answer and let the subject drop.

The problem wasn't going away. But one of the great things about this new inexplicable relationship was that there was no need to rush.

TWO NIGHTS LATER, Jack stopped by Erica's office on his way from a meeting at the Capitol, hoping he'd be in time to catch her. They didn't have plans to see each other, since she had Kevin that night, but he wanted to say hello before she went home to her son.

Because it was after five, most of the offices were silent, which gave him the chance to find hers without raising speculation. Erica guarded her privacy carefully, which was the reason he'd never been to her office before. Or at least one of the reasons.

He wasn't all that eager to have their relationship become fodder for office gossip, either. Other than that first week in Washington several months ago, back when they'd thought those few days an anomaly, they'd stayed away from restaurants where she might be recognized by politicians and their staff.

With loosened tie—one of Jack's complaints about his new job was the business attire he had to wear every day, rather than the casual clothes he was used to—he noticed the light still on under her door and approached with a smile. The door was open a crack. He knocked and pushed it open.

She was standing in the middle of the room, her back to her desk, facing a part of the room Jack couldn't see at first. She was wearing an olive skirt and jacket with a cream-colored blouse. Her shoes matched her suit. And her legs…they were magnificent.

"Hey," he greeted her.

Erica's head jerked toward the door, her eyes surprised, as though she hadn't heard him knock. "Jack!"

"I was hoping you'd still be here," he said, sauntering toward her. It had been two days since he'd seen her. Touched her.

Two days of trying not to think about all the unanswered questions.

He'd missed her.

"Jack." She took a step back, glancing uncomfortably over her shoulder.

That was when Jack first noticed the couch the door frame had hidden from view.

He recognized the man sitting there from press photos. And probably a television interview or two. Senator Jefferson Cooley.

"Jack," Erica said for the third time. "This is Jefferson. Jeff, Jack."

The older man rose from the couch, extended a hand. Because he had absolutely no idea what else to do, Jack shook it.

"Good to meet you," Cooley said. "Erica speaks highly of you."

Prepared to dislike the man, Jack was a bit perturbed to find that he couldn't. He found himself impressed with his dignity, instead. Apparently nothing about his relationship with Erica was going to be easy.

"Probably not as highly as she speaks of you," Jack admitted honestly. He eyed Jefferson Cooley, knowing it was ridiculous to feel any jealousy at all when *he* was the man Erica was sleeping with.

He hadn't expected the guilt, either, but that he accepted.

"I'm sorry," he said, backing up, glancing from one to the other, avoiding Erica's eyes. "I didn't realize you were busy, Erica. I'll talk to you later."

It was also ridiculous to be disappointed when Erica didn't call him back, try to stop him, tell him he was welcome to stay.

Must be his night for the ridiculous.

Walking purposefully toward one of his new favorite pubs, he tried not to wonder what was going on in that quiet suite of offices between an ex-husband and wife who were obviously still fond of each other.

He hated the fact that he had no right to ask. And no right to Erica at all.

CHAPTER FOURTEEN

"MOM? WHERE ARE YOU?" Kevin walked slowly into Erica's room Wednesday night. She was standing in front of the closet, cursing herself for forgetting to pick up the laundry. The presence of Jack in her life was not kind to her daily routine—the mundane details of living.

Her black stretch pants weren't in her closet. Neither were two of her favorite pairs of slacks.

"I'm right here, sport," she said when he missed her by the closet and headed toward the adjoining bathroom. "What's up?"

Dressed in slacks and a polo shirt—the tie having been disposed of in deference to the casual evening he was going to spend with his father and Pamela—he passed her four-poster bed and sat on the love seat in the corner of her room. The same place Jefferson had been sitting when she'd told him she was pregnant with another man's child.

"I don't want to go to Daddy's tonight."

Dread seeped through her. "Why not?" she asked, abandoning the closet to join her son on the love seat. She had to restrain herself from pulling him onto her lap. Lately he'd decided he was getting too grown-up to be cuddled. The change was one of many that were slowly breaking her heart.

"It was better when Daddy came here."

"He still comes here." He'd been there just a couple of nights ago when she'd gone out with Jack.

The little boy frowned. "Not with the whole family here."

Oh, sweetie, how can I help you understand something when I can't understand it myself? How do I keep you from hurting when I'm hurting so badly, too?

"Our family is changing, Kev," she said. "It's getting bigger, with more houses and more people. You go to Daddy's sometimes so you can be part of both houses and get to know Pamela, too."

The boy was silent, his feet sticking out in front of him.

"You like Pamela, don't you, sport?"

Since Erica genuinely liked the other woman, she figured Kevin would have a hard time not doing so. He shrugged.

"I know she's really fond of you," Erica continued, loving her son so much that selling him on her replacement didn't even faze her at the moment. "She pays lots of attention to you and she's always nice, isn't she?"

He shrugged again.

"You've said Pamela talks to you and tells you neat stuff."

"She does." He nodded solemnly, his mature expression so at odds with the babyish contours of his face. "I guess I like her." The admission came reluctantly.

"So why don't you want to go?"

He looked up at her, his lower lip starting to quiver. "I don't want to leave you all alone."

"Oh, Kev, it's okay," she said, pulling him into her arms whether that complied with his new rules or not. "I'm fine."

He shook his head, though she noticed he didn't try to pull away. Too needy to resist taking advantage of the moment, she drew him fully onto her lap, sitting back so he could lay his head against her, just as he'd done countless times during the first four years of his life.

If they were out late or they'd spent long hours campaigning, if they were at a movie, even at home on the couch, he used to climb up on her lap and fall asleep that way. It was one of the memories Erica cherished most. The feel of that warm body against hers. Trusting her.

Something Jack had missed out on.

"You love Daddy and me," he said. "And if the nucl'ar war comes, there won't be a soldier here to save you."

Swallowing back tears, she put a hand gently against the side of his face. "There isn't going to be a nuclear war, Kevin," she said, trying for a tone that was light enough to calm his fears and solemn enough to reassure him that she was taking him seriously.

"If Daddy doesn't win and keep the munitions away, there could be a war, Mom," he said, such a little man-child. "They don't have so many armies and guns and generals anymore like they used to. Just some guys get mad and fight." The words were so matter-of-fact she nearly cried.

"It isn't easy to get nuclear weapons, Kevin. There are all kinds of safeguards." She repeated what had become almost litany to her and Jefferson, hoping that someday her little boy would relax and allow himself to believe it. "And besides, we have satellites all over the world taking pictures of all the other countries and their weapons and military. And taking pictures of the sky, too, so that no one can get close enough to us to drop a bomb on us."

"But they could send nucl'ar stuff in envelopes with mailmen."

"No, Kev, it doesn't work like that."

He sighed, shook his head, as though he alone understood the monumental problems they all faced. She'd give her life to find a way to convince him that his world was safe, that he didn't have to assume responsibility for anyone, even himself. That he could be a child...

"Anyways, I don't want to go."

He *had* to go. He needed Jefferson.

"Would it help any if you knew I wasn't going to be here alone while you're gone?"

He sat up, frowning. "Who's coming here?"

"No one," she said. "I'm going out."

"To a business dinner?"

"No."

He played with the Madonna on the chain around her neck. "Where, then?"

"On a date."

"With a man?"

Erica tried not to laugh at the disbelieving tone in his voice. "Yes, sport, that's what a date is. A woman and a man who enjoy each other's company go out someplace to spend some time together."

"Do you get to laugh?"

Her heart caught at the odd question. "Yes."

"Do I know the man?" He was sitting on her knees. Erica wished his head was still against her, where he couldn't see her expression. She couldn't risk his peace of mind by letting him know how badly she hurt, how painful it was to tell him about the man who'd fathered him as though Jack was nothing more than a stranger on the street.

Hurt, too, because Jack knew nothing about this precious and oh-so-unusual son.

"You met him once," she said lightly. "Remember at the beginning of the summer, that day you thought that man was going to take our spot out on the mall?"

"The one who ate Daddy's sandwich."

"Yes, that's the one. His name is Jack, remember?"

He gazed at her, unsmiling, his dark-brown eyes wide. "He worked at the FBI."

"Yes."

"Doesn't he like me?"

"Of course he likes you!" Erica said, shocked. "Where on earth did that come from?"

"'Cause Daddy stayed here before so you could eat dinner with Jack 'stead of me and Daddy. And now you're going to date him again without me. Maybe he didn't think I chewed my food good at the picnic."

How had Kevin even thought of such a thing?

"He likes you, Kevin," she said. "He was out of town for a long time after our picnic, and now I just see him when you're with Daddy because I don't want to waste any of the time I get to spend with you."

It wasn't the whole truth. But it was as much of it as her son needed to hear.

"But Daddy has Pamela when I'm with him. Is he wasting his time with me?"

Throat thick, Erica felt her choices closing in on her. "Of course not."

"Maybe Jack should come to our house for dinner, like Pamela comes to Daddy's new house."

The precarious control she had was slipping. "Maybe."

Kevin slid off her lap. "Ask him tonight, okay, Mom?" he asked. "I have some FBI questions to ask him."

With that, the boy marched purposefully from the room to collect his overnight bag.

Suddenly she was the one who didn't want him to go to Jefferson's. She wanted to spirit him away and live with him in some imaginary place where happily-ever-after wasn't just a cruel illusion found in fairy tales and romance novels.

"YOU'RE AWFULLY QUIET. What are you thinking?"

They were sitting on Jack's bed, Erica wearing nothing but a shirt of Jack's. She'd gone from Mommy to seductive lover in less than two hours. She loved both lives. But hated living a double one.

Wearing the nylon exercise shorts he'd pulled out of a drawer to answer the door to the person delivering their Chinese food, Jack lounged on his side. He leaned on an elbow, facing her. The remains of their dinner and its cardboard containers were on the bed between them as he waited for her answer.

Just moments before, he'd fed her rice with chopsticks. He'd handled them as confidently as he did everything he touched—hostage-takers, training schools, her. It was no wonder she was so addicted to him.

He shifted slightly. "Tell me," he said more urgently.

"I'm just having problems seeing my way clear."

He didn't move, not anything perceptible, but she felt Jack brace himself.

"I can't find a picture that works. It's the only way I can explain it."

His brow furrowed in puzzlement. "What kind of picture are you looking for?"

"My life," she said, relaxing just a little. Whatever happened, at least they were talking about it. "I have two distinct and completely separate pictures in my head. There's my life with you. And then there's the rest of my life."

"And why is that bad?"

"Because it's only one life, Jack. I'm only one person and yes, I play different roles, but they're all *me*."

"I don't see the problem with that. You play your roles in different places at different times. Everyone does." He sat up, ran a finger lightly down her calf. "When you're at the office, you're Senator Jefferson Cooley's communications director. At home, you're Kevin's mother. With me you're…"

"What?" she asked, meeting his gaze because she had no other choice. "What am I?"

"My lover."

Desire melted through her.

Although she wasn't sure exactly what that answer meant…

"For how long?"

The question wasn't fair. She knew that. It crossed the line they'd drawn. The line between today and forever, between enjoyment and commitment.

"For as long as it lasts."

She liked that answer, too. Yet she probably shouldn't have.

"Okay, so say it lasts a year."

"Okay."

"During that year, the people in my life are going to be affected by my association with you."

"Why do they have to be?"

She had to think about that for a minute. "The people I work with—some of us have been together for more than ten years. They're my friends. They care about me."

Jack's face creased into a slow intimate smile. "I'd expect them to," he said.

"Yes, but the fact that they care imposes certain obligations. Take tomorrow, for instance. When I go in, they'll ask me what I did tonight. They always do. I've been vague one time too many, and they've guessed there's a man in my life. They're insisting on meeting him. Checking him out, as good friends do."

She'd meant to tell him that her son was suffering due to his exclusion from their relationship. But this was true, as well.

"And would it be so terrible if I met them?"

"You have to understand," she said, trying to understand herself why the prospect frightened her so much. "Since Jeff left me, they've been very protective. Worried. They're thrilled to think I've found someone, but they won't relax until I'm safely..."

"Married?" He didn't look away.

So she did. "I don't know. No. But considering how often we see each other, they're going to think there's some kind of commitment here. You'll get invitations to things and then there'll be holidays when you'll be expected to be around and—" She stopped, glanced back at him. "It all gets so complicated."

And that was without Kevin. Oh, man, what was she doing?

"Hey." Setting aside the remains of their meal, he pulled her hand until she fell forward across him. His arms closed around her. "Don't panic," he said. "We're in control here."

"But don't you see? It's becoming a commitment whether we say it can be one or not."

"Not if we don't let it." He kissed her briefly.

"I don't know why you came into my life," he said softly. "I don't know why you alone give my life a dimension it's never had before. I don't know why I met you after Melissa and not before. I only know two things." His face was an inch from hers, his body, already hardening, pressed against her. "First, I know I can't change the circumstances that have shaped us into the people we are. And second, I know that while you and I are still getting along so incredibly well, we'd be fools to let this slip away."

But they might not be getting along well in another week or another month. She knew that as well as he did. Much better, in fact, considering the secret she was keeping.

And he was right. She could see the dark clouds looming in the future, but the truth was that for now—for as long as she and Jack shared this ability to make each other's lives so much more than they could possibly be alone—she had to continue seeing him.

Pushing him over, she slid on top of him—and almost came when he uttered a long, sensual groan of rapture. Came not only from her own ecstasy, though there was definitely that, but from the headiness of bringing him his.

As difficult as life with Jack was proving to be, he could always make her feel better. Help her regain control. When he talked to her, she always felt confident that no matter what, she could cope.

Until the next time.

And that was the bad part. There was always a next time.

JEFF WASN'T SURPRISED when Erica sought him out the next afternoon. Without preamble she walked briskly into his office, closed the door and sat on the couch. He joined her.

He'd do anything for her. It had always been like that. But as he sat there with her, ready to help her in whatever way necessary, he had a flash of Pamela in his living room the night before. She'd been laughing at something he'd said, looking at him with such unabashed desire in her eyes, he'd wanted to take her right there in the middle of the floor. He had to amend his initial thought: he'd do *almost* anything for Erica.

"Kevin told me you asked Jack to come to dinner," he said, trying to make this easier for her.

Head slightly bent, she gazed up at him, her brown eyes filled with torment and that odd core of strength that had always attracted him. "I was supposed to," she said. "I didn't."

"There's a problem between you?"

"Other than the fact that he has a son he knows nothing about?" she asked, clearly angry with herself.

He had to get off this roller-coaster ride. He was too damned old. "I told you to tell him."

She shook her head. "Of course I can't tell him! And you know why."

Thinking of his son's vulnerabilities and fears, Jefferson nodded.

"Part of the reason I didn't ask him is because there's no commitment between Jack and me. How can I introduce him into Kevin's life knowing that at some point he'll disappear? Especially considering how badly Kevin's taken the divorce."

"You're sure he'll disappear?" Jeff asked. And felt ashamed for the brief flash of gratitude he felt at that thought.

"Doesn't everybody at some point or other?" she asked. "First Shane. And then…" She bowed her head for a moment. Composed, she looked up again. "You were going to love me forever, Jeff, and even you couldn't stay the course. No one's ever adored me like you did. Not that I'm blaming you," she said quickly. "I know what I did was horrible. I know it's my fault, but don't you see? If I can't even rely on *myself* to stay true, when fidelity and trust are more important to me than anything, how can I possibly rely on anyone else?"

He could argue with her, but he'd been a politician a long time. He knew when debate was the wrong choice. "Okay, you've said Kevin's security was part of the reason. What's the rest of it?"

"How can I bring the two of them together, knowing what I do, and not tell them? It makes the lie so much bigger."

"You're a strong woman, Erica. You'll do what you have to do." He spoke with conviction.

"What if he guesses?"

"It would've happened by now."

"Kevin might do something, you know, hereditary, that might give him a clue. Maybe someone in his family had the same birthmark that's on Kevin's ribs."

"There's no reason for him to suspect anything, Erica." Jefferson hated to see her twisting herself in knots. And hated how much the whole thing was twisting him, too. "You were married when you were with Jack. I'm assuming he didn't know that Kevin couldn't possibly have been mine...."

Her forthright glance comforted him far more than was warranted. "No," she said. "Of course not."

She'd never know what a salve her loyalty was to him.

"According to what you've told me," he said in a voice that was as reassuring as he could make it, "having a child is so far out of the realm of what Jack Shaw believes he can handle, he'd avoid the truth if his name was written on the birth certificate."

She nodded. Pulled a tissue out of the box on the coffee table, wrapped and unwrapped it around her index finger.

"And how do I have him in my house—our house—when he's the reason you aren't there?"

"He's not the reason."

"Of course he is."

"No." Jefferson shook his head. "Jack was only a symptom. He wasn't the cause."

"I don't want him in our house," she admitted, her face lined with distress. "I'm afraid to have him that close."

Feeling every one of his sixty-five years, Jefferson leaned forward, his back aching right along with his heart.

"You're in love with him."

The shocked look in her eyes was all the answer he needed. "No!" The denial was vehement.

But it didn't change the truth. She might not be ready to admit she was in love with Jack Shaw, but he read a reluctant recognition in her eyes.

He knew her well. Sometimes almost better than she knew herself—a condition more painful to him than he could ever have imagined. There were times he could sense so clearly what she was feeling. Yet, because of her love for another man, he'd been rendered powerless to help her.

"What's the matter with me, Jeff?" she cried. "How can I need and want him so badly and want out at the same time? How could I have been with him in the first place when I loved you?"

He had to be honest.

"Loving me is safe, honey," he said, sitting back. He didn't allow himself to take hold of the soft slim hands torturing that tissue, didn't let himself touch her at all. "You love me, but you were never in love with me. The *in love* part is what makes you so vulnerable. It ups the ante incomparably. Instead of being a force that drives you, I'm a steady warmth in the background. Older. Safe. In some ways, giving you the same sense of security a father would."

These truths were painful to him, humiliating. They'd been so long in coming. If only he'd recognized them ten years ago. If only...

"I'm just a haven for you, Erica."

"No!" She dropped to the floor in front of him. "You are a wonderful giving man, Jeff. I care about you for that, not because I'm looking for a place to hide."

He lifted a hand to run it through her hair and stopped himself. "I know," he said. "But the ability to hide was a bonus you couldn't resist."

"I don't believe that!"

He hadn't really expected her to. Not yet. It would take a while. She'd think everything through, just as she always did, in her own time. And eventually, she'd arrive at the convictions that would guide the rest of her life.

Just as he had.

He hoped the process wasn't as painful for her as it had been for him. His real hope should be that she'd have Jack to help her through it, the way he had Pamela. But right then, sitting there alone with her at his feet—probably for the last time—Jeff just couldn't be that generous.

At that moment he hated Jack Shaw.

Mostly because he had to hate *someone,* and Jack Shaw was a hell of a lot easier to hate than Erica or himself.

CHAPTER FIFTEEN

"ERICA, RUDY WALLACE here."

"Hi, Rudy." The snake. Another man she'd trusted who'd—

No. She wasn't going to let life, or her emotional exhaustion, make her bitter.

"Everyone wants to hear what the senator has to say about the nuclear weapons bill that's being introduced next month," the reporter said, forgoing the banter that used to be so natural between them.

"This office has released several statements—"

"Yeah, yeah. The stuff you and your staff have written, I know," Rudy muttered, his vigilance, at least, status quo. "And Senator Cooley has given the requisite speeches, all nicely written and all saying the same things. What everyone wants is straight answers to the real questions. Senator Cooley's taking some hard hits on this one. What does he stand to gain? Who's backing him that we don't know about? Who's he backing in return?"

Erica almost smiled. Sometimes the game was fun. But not with Rudy. Not anymore. "Shall I fax you a copy of the senator's most recent speech?" she asked. It was Friday. Two days' respite lay just ahead.

"Cut the crap, Erica. Your halo's finally slipped a bit in the past month. You've been in Washington your whole life. You know when it's time to give a little to protect your hide."

Erica's hands started to shake. "You wouldn't be trying to blackmail me, would you, Rudy?" she asked calmly.

"No. Of course not, Erica," he said mockingly. "But a friendly word of advice." His voice was deadly serious. "It's a lot more pleasant to have friends and play nice in this city than it is to have enemies and walk alone."

She barely heard him over the pounding of the blood through her veins. The thinly veiled threat pushed her to the edge of a cliff she'd been adamantly avoiding.

For the first time she had to consider the possibility that she might not have a choice about jumping off.

She might have to tell Jack that he was Kevin's father.

"I HAD NO IDEA she was this far gone."

Jack's attention was not on the distraught father who spoke quietly beside him Friday afternoon. He was completely focused on the woman behind the locked bathroom door.

"Let's think about this, Molly," he said softly.

"You don't want to hurt your daughter. You love her far too much to do that."

"I do-o-o-o." Molly Gaston wailed pathetically, a testimony to her frantic mental state. "I love you, Katie, you know that, don't you?"

Jack listened carefully for a response, for any sign that the eight-year-old was still alive. He heard silence.

There were no windows in the bathroom. A team of Washington police crisis specialists was standing by, ready to rush the door if Jack made the call. That would be his last resort. The door crashing down on her could easily drive the unbalanced wife of Dr. Talbot Gaston to one last act of desperation.

Killing their daughter.

"I never would've left Katie here after telling Molly I wanted a divorce if I'd thought for a second that she'd turn on her. Katie's the one person I know Molly loves."

Gaston's face was white, pinched. An orthopedic surgeon, the tall, athletically built forty-year-old man didn't appear confident and capable. He looked like a scared kid. Beaten.

"Talk to her, Gaston," Jack said. They'd been at this for more than an hour. His instincts were telling him they didn't have much time left.

Gaston crouched down, his face inches from the doorknob. "What do I say?" he whispered. There was desperation in his eyes.

"Can someone call my priest, please?" Molly's voice was weak. "Please?"

"I'll go," Gaston said.

Jack grabbed his arm. "No. No clergy."

"But she asked—"

"No clergy," Jack said quietly, but with steel. "She's trying to legitimize her desire for self-destruction. If she finds absolution for what she knows is wrong, she'll act on it. Talk to her."

There was a rustle on the floor behind the door. And then a sob.

A childish sob. Katie was still alive.

"Thank God," Gaston's voice broke before he quickly controlled himself.

Jack pulled him in front of the door again.

Molly was beyond reason. Beyond professional help at the moment. She needed someone who could reach the innermost places inside her and help her find a remnant of the woman she once was.

"Tell her you had no idea she cared this much. That you'd really like another chance to talk to her. To make this work for both of you."

Gaston nodded. "I'll stay married to her forever if that's what it takes to keep Katie safe."

"Worry about that later," Jack said. "Right now, let's get your daughter out of there."

Gaston broke once more, one sob, and then straightened. Jack wasn't surprised by the strength, the assurance and concern in the man's voice as he spoke to his mentally ill wife. Gaston was fighting for the life of his only child.

Something Jack would've given his life to have had the chance to do.

AN HOUR AND A HALF later, hands in his pockets because they didn't feel quite steady, Jack approached the Hart Senate Office Building. This late on a Friday he expected the building to be deserted, but hoped he might get lucky one more time and find Erica still in her office.

His footsteps loud on the tile floor, he rounded a corner. Her office was halfway down the hall just ahead. It was no big deal if she wasn't there. He was fine.

Of course, he'd looked forward to relating the afternoon's incident, as he always did when he experienced something like this. Talking to Erica helped him exorcise it, insofar as that was possible. He recalled Gaston's horror upon arriving to find his wife locked in their downstairs bathroom with his daughter and a butcher knife. Thank God he and Gaston had managed to talk her down.

Erica's light was on, he could see the reflection in the hall outside her door. Increasing his pace, Jack made up his mind. Even if Cooley was there with her, he wasn't leaving.

He almost strode right in and hauled her up from that impressive leather chair behind the cherry desk and made love to her then and there. Door open and all. He needed her to rescue him from darkness. Needed her to share life and joy with him, to wipe away the threat of death and the stench of desperation.

"Hi," he said, instead, leaning against the doorjamb as though he'd done nothing more that day than write curriculum.

Erica looked up from her computer screen, her face blank for the second it took her to recognize him. "Jack!" she said. She met him halfway for a kiss that righted his world.

"Hi!"

Jerking back, stunned, Jack turned to see a miniature version of Jefferson walk into the room as though he owned the place. "I was in the bathroom, but I'm back now."

"Kevin, you remember Jack?" Erica's voice was slightly choked.

"Yep. Hi, Jack," Kevin said. "Me and Mom are working on a important speech for my dad to give. It's about not making more nucl'ar munitions. You know anything about that?"

"Not much," Jack said. Not as much as Jefferson Cooley, certainly. And even if he was an expert, he didn't think he'd admit that to Erica's troubled son.

While he'd been talking to the boy, she'd returned to her seat behind her desk.

"You going to be here long?" Jack asked her.

She frowned at the pages spread close to her computer. "Maybe not," she said. "Kevin and I were supposed to be going out for pizza tonight, but some new statistics came in that substantially change Jefferson's arguments in a speech he's giving in the morning. I'm working on the press release that's going out right afterward.''

She and Jack glanced at Kevin at the same time. The boy had climbed onto a chair beside Erica's computer and was looking at a book on his lap. It was open to a full-page map of the United States.

''Do you know where all the old nucl'ar munitions plants are, Jack?'' he asked. ''Mom says she's not sure.''

''I'm not sure, either,'' Jack said. ''But I do know how to make a bunch of different bird whistles. You know how to whistle yet?''

''No. I got some cards here. You want to play war?''

''I never liked that game,'' Jack said. ''But I know slapjack. You want to try that?'' Jack couldn't quite believe he was asking the boy this.

''Okay,'' Kevin said. ''Just until Mom's done with our work and we go to get pizza. You want to come for pizza?'' The miniature man had climbed down from his chair, cards in hand, and was heading toward the coffee table in front of the couch. Almost without conscious thought, Jack followed him.

''I'd like that if your mom won't mind,'' Jack said. He glanced over at Erica, expecting her to be following the interplay, and was surprised to find her engrossed in her computer.

"She won't mind," Kevin said. "I know she likes to eat with you because she does it a lot."

Probably because the afternoon's incident was still fresh in his mind, Jack kept interposing his feelings about the Gaston girl on Erica's son. As though the boy needed to be rescued. Not from a disturbed mother, but from something potentially as dangerous. Little Kevin Cooley was being held hostage by his own mind.

Feeling like a freshman on his first day of high school, Jack spent the next half hour playing cards with a five-year-old boy. Nothing felt right. Or natural. Yet he had no choice but to stay.

Kind of like people being drawn to a bad car accident. No one ever wanted to be there. Bystanders knew it was going to bother them, stick with them long after they'd gone on their way. And yet, they couldn't *not* look.

To Jack, Erica's son was a bad car accident.

ERICA CALLED JACK on Sunday afternoon. Said she had something to talk to him about. Kevin was with his father.

Jack suggested they take a cab down to the Potomac River. When he'd been out riding his new bike the previous weekend, he'd discovered a paved trail that ran for miles through beautiful woods along the river.

"I've in-line skated this trail many times, but never walked it," Erica said as they started out.

Jack took her hand. "I used to skate in Central Park."

"You have skates?"

"No, there was a place down by the park where you could rent them."

"We should get you some. I'd love to have someone to go with."

The future implied in that statement relaxed him a bit. "So what is it you needed to talk to me about?"

They'd been out on Saturday—took in a theater production at the Kennedy Center, which had been impressive, but the best part of the evening had been going to an out-of-the-way pub where they'd shared appetizers and beer afterward, laughing, talking about their most embarrassing moments, their first dates, their worst dates—all things they'd never had time for in the past.

It took him a second to realize she wasn't answering his question. Senses tuned, he braced himself for something he wasn't going to like.

"Erica?"

"It's about Kevin."

Jack breathed a little easier. At least it wasn't about them.

"More problems?" Jack really felt for her. Kevin was an engaging little guy. If Jack had ever had a son, he'd probably have been nothing like Erica's boy. He'd have had no manners, and no idea how to hold an intelligent conversation, either.

"I need your help, Jack."

Jack felt on edge, but his reply was nonetheless instantaneous. "Tell me what I can do."

"I need you to come over for dinner."

"Name the time," he told her.

"Kevin will be there."

"Fine," he said quickly, trying to disguise his reaction. Being with Kevin bothered him. A lot. Because he liked the little guy far too much.

Erica stopped, gazing up at him. "You're really okay with this?"

He swallowed, met her eyes, then looked out over the riverbank, and back. "He's a part of you, Erica," he said, ignoring the driving compulsion he felt to help the boy. "I want to know as many parts of you as I can."

Jack, starting to walk again, stopped when Erica didn't budge. "He's a person in his own right," she said, "not just a part of me. He has thoughts and feelings and needs."

"I know."

A couple of skaters, in full head, wrist and knee gear whizzed by.

"He thinks you don't like him because you changed your mind about going out for pizza with us the other night."

Without warning a picture of that pudgy little boy in South Dakota came to mind, the shocked look in his eyes when the bullet burst through him, telling him forevermore that not everyone in the world loved him. Or would protect him.

"I liked him a lot."

"He doesn't understand why you aren't as involved with his life as Pamela is."

This time when he started to walk, she came with him. Jack was tempted to release her hand, to travel on his own—but this was Erica, and he wasn't ready to let go yet.

"It's only because he's with Jefferson every time we're together that he hasn't seen me."

Jack wanted to pretend that that was wholly and completely true. But...

"We only see each other when Kevin's with Jefferson so *you* don't have to see him."

The damaging words came softly, whispering across the Sunday breeze. Before he could respond—not that he knew what to say, a group of cyclists appeared behind them, serious ones, judging from the skintight shorts, shirts and the helmets they were wearing. Jack thought longingly of his expensive new high-performance bike.

He couldn't bear the thought that he was hurting any kid. Especially Erica's. Kevin was one of the most compelling little kids he'd ever met. And he'd met lots of kids, far too many, in his career.

"So when's dinner?" he asked. Sometime between now and then he'd find a way to relieve the panic in his chest.

She stopped again. "Kevin's sharp, Jack," she said, moving off the path as another cyclist sped past.

"It took me about ten seconds to figure that out."

"You have to be honest with me." Her beautiful brown eyes implored him. "He'll figure out in no time if you don't want to be with him. I can't afford to expose him to that. If you can be comfortable with my son, then I need you there. If you can't, then I don't want you."

I don't want you. The words seared him.

"I'll be okay."

He would be. Somehow.

APPROACHING THE BUILDING with brown bag in hand, Jack didn't look any different from any other man who might've come calling on a woman and her son. At least that was what Erica decided when she peeked through the window in the den and saw him coming down the street. He was wearing gray slacks and a white polo shirt that deftly outlined the muscles in his upper arms.

She wondered what was in the bag.

And how she was going to get through the next couple of hours. Her stomach had been churning since yesterday afternoon, when Jack had insisted they have this dinner right away.

He'd said they shouldn't make Kevin suffer under misapprehensions a day longer than necessary. Much as she wanted to find a reason to postpone tonight, she hadn't been able to argue with him. So here she was, on Monday night, still in the navy suit she'd worn all day, with Italian takeout in the oven, waiting to bring her lover into the home she'd shared with her ex-husband.

And still shared with the son he didn't know was his.

"He's here, sport," she told the little boy, who'd already checked the dining room twice to make sure he'd set out the napkins and silverware exactly as he'd been taught. His hair, the same shade as Jack's, had been neatly combed and he'd put on his tie an hour before. "You want to get the door?"

"Yeah." He waited in the archway between the den and the foyer.

Erica's heart broke for the tiny soldier so determined to fight battles. She'd tried to get him to forgo the tie, to put on one of the T-shirts he used to love.

But he'd been adamant.

Erica was afraid to know what was going on in her son's mind, how he'd convinced himself that he needed to be a man. Why he felt he wasn't entitled to be a little boy.

The second Jack stepped into the condo, Erica was terrified. But so, so glad. The place hadn't been complete without him in it, *they* hadn't been complete, as a couple, until he saw where she spent her private time.

Like a tour guide, Kevin showed Jack around the condo before he'd even had a chance to say hello. Or dispense with his bag.

"This is where I do my work," he said, indicating a stool pulled up to Erica's desk at the far end of the den. "Mom does hers over there." He pointed to her chair. "Come this way, please."

He led Jack through the condo, talking constantly in his childish voice with its adult intonations. Erica tried to catch Jack's eye, to apologize, shrug, thank him, tell him hello, but his attention was completely on the boy in front of him. Too nervous to follow them, Erica stayed in the den, opening a bottle of beer for Jack and pouring herself a glass of white wine.

"That's my mom's room," she heard Kevin say. Heat spread through her and she took a sip of wine. She'd have to get a grip if she was going to survive this evening.

Jack there in her home. Standing right outside the bedroom that had hidden so many of her tears and secrets.

"And this is my room." Kevin's voice rose, and he sounded, just a little, like the young boy he was.

Jack there with her son. Their son. *His son.*

Kevin marched back into the den importantly, glancing over his shoulder at his guest. "What's in your bag?"

"It's a surprise." Finally Jack met her eyes.

And the smile she saw in those depths took her breath away.

"Oh," Kevin said. "You want to sit down?" He climbed into Jeff's chair, leaving the opposite one for Jack.

"Sure," Jack said, and then, "thank you," to Erica as she handed him the bottle of beer. He turned back to Kevin. "Your mom make you guys use coasters here?" he asked.

"Yeah," Kevin jumped down immediately, got a couple of the leather coasters from under the coffee table and set one out for Jack. He put another one by his chair.

Erica poured her son a glass of cranberry juice and placed it beside him, smiling when Kevin forgot to say thank you, like any other little boy.

Kevin was trying not to stare at the brown bag Jack had sitting on his lap. And failing.

"Don't you want to know who the surprise is for?" Jack asked, his attention on Kevin.

He'd make a wonderful father. The unexpected thought caught her completely off guard. In another time, another life, Jack would've been able to give so much. Just in the few times she'd seen him with Kevin she'd noticed the natural affinity he seemed to have with children.

Or was it just his son?

Was she robbing them both of something vital by keeping her secret? In trying to protect them, was she hurting them, instead? Inflicting more pain where she tried so hard to bring happiness?

Or would telling her secret cause the greater pain?

And what about Jefferson?

Wineglass in hand, Erica sat on the sofa perpendicular to them, looking out the wall of windows across the room. There'd been many nights when Jefferson seemed mesmerized by those lights. Right now she wished they'd have the same effect on her.

"Yes, I want to know," Kevin was saying. "If you want to tell me, that is."

"Why don't you guess?"

Unable to help herself, Erica turned, watching them.

She watched their son, waiting to see how'd he react to Jack's challenge. In the old days, the days before Jefferson left, Kevin would've been jumping up and down with excitement. He would've been determined to figure it out.

"I don't know," he said now. "It's okay if you don't want to tell me."

Oh, Kev, come on little buddy, you don't have to be this way.

"That's just it," Jack said, leaning toward Kevin, almost as though sharing something confidential. "I *want* to tell, but it's more fun if you guess first. Can you hurry it up a little?"

He was good.

"Well—" Kevin's brow furrowed, and his eyes were glued to the bag. "It's pro'bly not flowers for my mom."

"Probably not."

"Might be candy, though."

"Maybe."

"But only if you're a guy who's not good at giving ladies presents."

Jack's head tilted back, his hair brushing over his collar. "Why's that?"

Kevin bounced his legs against the chair. "'Cause ladies like all that flowery paper and bows and stuff that makes a present hard to open."

Jack looked at Erica, eyebrows raised. "He's been taught well."

Erica smiled, fighting a flood of guilt.

She was desperate to maintain her precarious hold on all the pieces of her life—by keeping all her roles separate and distinct. And yet she needed Jack to know the truth just as badly. She was only beginning to realize how much Kevin could gain from this man.

But then, if Jack knew, he wouldn't be sitting there so easy and relaxed, teasing her son about a bag.

And Kevin. Could she risk her son's emotional health because of her own need for absolution?

"So are you good at giving ladies presents?" Kevin asked.

Jack nodded. "Very good."

"So who's the surprise for?" Kevin's voice rose on the last word. He'd scooted to the edge of the chair, his legs dangling, swinging.

Erica stared out the window again, trying not to let things matter so much. She took a sip of the wine she'd barely touched.

"I don't know," Jack said. "I forget."

Erica turned back in time to see him peering into the shopping bag. He looked up, glanced between Kevin and Erica, and then back down. Very carefully he refolded the top of the bag.

Kevin's face fell and his feet stopped moving, but his eyes were filled with anticipation as he stared at that bag. They got bigger and bigger as the bag moved his way.

"I think it's for you," Jack said, when the bag was close enough for Kevin to reach. "Seems to me it'll only work for someone your size."

Off the seat and on the floor—where Erica hadn't seen her son in months—Kevin eagerly tore open the bag. She and Jeff had given him ten presents for his birthday and he hadn't shown even a shadow of this enthusiasm for one of them.

But then, they'd been too worried about him to be playful, as Jack had just been.

"Rollerblades!" The boy hollered, pulling the skates out of their wrapping. "Look, Mommy! Just like yours!"

Erica was unaware that her son even wanted skates. She made all the right sounds, said all the right words, wore the right smiles as she congratulated Kevin on such a great gift and watched him pull off the constricting dress shoes and work his way into the skates. She knew better than to try to help. Kevin would just tell her he was all grown up now.

However, he didn't say that when Jack slid down to the floor, leaning back against his chair as though he was only getting more comfortable, and quietly lent an unobtrusive hand the one or two times Kevin had difficulty fastening the skates.

"They're too big," Jack said once, to which Kevin replied, "No, I like them that way."

"Having a little room to grow is good," Jack said, considering. "Maybe if you just wear a couple pairs of socks…"

The boy nodded. "Yeah," he said. "That'll do it for sure."

"I've got some just like these," he told Kevin. "I figured you and your mom and I could all go down to the river and skate together."

"Cool!" the little boy said. "Did you hear that, Mommy?" Kevin didn't even look up. "We're going skating."

Erica heard. And was suffocating.

By dinnertime Kevin had collected himself, reverting to the man-child as he played host to their guest. But for a brief moment Erica had seen the little boy she'd lost when she lost Jeff.

Jack wasn't just a miracle worker in her life. He was in his son's, as well.

But if he knew the truth about them, they'd be anything but a miracle in his.

JACK PACED his apartment, the third bottle of beer sweating in his palm. He'd been home for hours, had left before Kevin could invite him to share in a bed-time story. He couldn't have handled that.

The skates had had their intended effect. They'd made Erica's son feel liked and wanted. They'd also freed Jack from the necessity of too many intimate meetings with the kid. Only so much conversation was possible when you were skating along the Potomac. And other than a possible broken bone or two, it was an activity that presented no real dangers. He'd bought the most expensive protective gear for Kevin. He'd told the boy that the only stipulation attached to their outings was that he always wear all the gear.

He'd been made more clearly aware of the challenges Erica was facing with her young son when the boy hadn't even groaned at the pronouncement.

Dinner had been okay. Jack looked out his front-room window, missing the lights, the activity, the distraction of Manhattan at night. Instead of crowds surging past, the sidewalk below was deserted. There was nothing to look at, nothing to take him away from his thoughts.

Not only had the meal with Kevin and his mom been a fairly quick one due to Kevin's bedtime, it had been entirely taken up with FBI questions that kept everything safe. Impersonal. Still, he'd been afforded a few glimpses into the mind of this boy Erica loved so much.

So why—hours later, in his air-conditioned apartment—was he sweating like a pig?

Jack's mind raced from one child to the next.

From sweet Courtney, whose baby smell he could still conjure up, to the myriad children he'd rescued over the years, to the one in South Dakota he hadn't been able to save, to amazing little Kevin. Trying to understand the events of his life, put everything neatly in place, he took another long swig of beer.

His thoughts weren't cooperating. The visions wouldn't go away. Children. It was always children. He cared about them. Understood them. Sometimes, when he was working, he could feel their fear, feel what they needed without their saying a word. It was as though he had a sixth sense. He just knew what to do or say to help them hold on until they could be rescued.

But he'd quit all that. Moved into a field where—with very few exceptions—there were only adults in his day. Left the world of children behind.

And now there was Kevin. Taunting him with something he couldn't understand. An affinity that made no sense.

How was he ever going to survive Erica's son?

Children. Their sweet faces and innocent spirits. Their trust. Courtney. That little body with a bullet hole through her chest.

Pain seared through him. Swift. Sharp. He couldn't

stand it. Couldn't stand to think of his baby daughter's helpless assaulted body.

No amount of alcohol in the world could ease his agony. Only forgetting could do that. And, oddly enough, Erica.

But Erica had a son.

Another child to pull at his tenuous compromise with grief.

He was going to have to take the kid in very small doses.

CHAPTER SIXTEEN

WITH HIS TIE DONE in a pretty good knot, Kevin put on his backpack and gritted his teeth so he wouldn't be scared. Today was the day of Mr. Terratruce's rally, he'd heard Mommy say so. He was sorta happy about that, happy that he'd finally be able to do something. And besides, the rally or party or whatever it was might be fun. At least more fun than sitting on the bench at Bobbie's party had been.

There'd probably be some food there that he liked. And maybe even some punch that he'd be allowed to drink.

He looked around his room one last time and saw his new skates on the floor by his closet. He was glad Jack had brought them last night. He wished he could take them, but figured he'd better not. Men didn't wear skates to parties, and today he had to be a man.

His daddy wasn't ever coming back home to live. He knew that 'cause now his mom was friends with Jack. Dads didn't move home when moms had friends who were men. And that meant if nucl'ar war came to his house, he was the one who'd have to save his mom.

But sometimes…he got so scared thinking about that war.

"Hmm, this is a rare treat."

Erica's skin tingled with renewed desire as Jack lay beside her on his bed. He'd barely gotten the spread pulled out of the way before they'd fallen to the sheets.

"You left too early last night," she said in a sultry voice, "I wasn't finished with dinner."

Lying on his side, propped on one elbow, Jack smiled and leaned in for a kiss. "Yeah, but lunch made up for it."

She'd called him that morning to see if he could meet her at his place for lunch. She'd promised to bring sandwiches. He was spending the morning looking at potential sites for the new crisis-training center and had been more than happy to comply.

Losing herself in another lingering kiss, Erica wished she could stay right where she was until she had all the answers that were eluding her. While Jack's presence in her life brought its own turmoil, it also brought her strength. And the confidence to believe she could get through the challenges facing her.

At least she felt that way when she was in his arms like this. With life's fire burning through her. Burning through him, too.

She pulled away and fell back against the pillows. "You left awfully early last night."

He opened his mouth as though he had something ready to say, and then didn't speak. Eventually he murmured, "I know."

"You were a big hit with Kevin."

Too big a hit.

"That was the skates, not me."

"The skates were great, Jack," she said, drawing the sheet up to her chin, "but it was you he was still talking about when he fell asleep."

The look on Jack's face changed, sobered. "He's a great kid."

"But you had trouble dealing with him, didn't you?"

"Nothing I can't handle."

Then why didn't he meet her eyes when he told her that?

"He's not going to rest now until we take him skating. You know that, don't you?"

And she wasn't going to rest, either. Never again as long as Kevin and Jack were in the same vicinity. She was terrified they'd find out about each other, terrified of the damage it would cause. And tormented by guilt for not telling them.

"I'm just wondering—" she reached over, ran a finger lightly down his chest "—at what point does time spent with him become too much? When does it get to the point where you *can't* handle it?"

"I don't know."

It wasn't a very reassuring answer. "So I just wait around whenever we're with Kevin and wonder if that'll be the time? And then you're gone from our lives?''

''No.'' His glance was warm. ''Let's not borrow trouble, okay?'' he said, taking hold of her hand. ''All we really know about is today, and today's looking pretty good to me.''

Because Erica needed as badly as he did to put aside the future and its risks, she didn't argue with him. But she couldn't stop worrying about her son. Not when his emotional well-being was at stake.

''I just don't want either of us to have any false expectations, you know?'' She met his eyes.

''But you're forgetting, there *are* no expectations.''

He was right, of course. The fact that he expected nothing of her—no promises she couldn't make or keep—made it possible for her to spend so much time with him. To be so open and available, emotionally, as well as physically.

Which was great for the two of them. But how did you bring a five-year-old emotionally fragile child into that situation and have him survive unscathed? Children had expectations. Period.

''Do you miss being a hostage negotiator?'' she asked after a few minutes of considering all she knew about Jack, trying to understand, to predict. To figure out how long she'd have with him. How she could best preserve what they had.

''No.''

He seemed mighty focused on the patterns decorating the sheet. He was tracing the same one over and over with his forefinger.

"You don't regret your decision to quit?" But he *could* regret the decision at any time. And be gone. Leaving her—and Kevin—to cope alone.

Jack frowned. "I'm certain I made the right decision."

Because there seemed to be so much he wasn't saying, she waited, hands folded across her chest, hoping he'd elaborate.

"It was time," he admitted, his eyes shadowed as he glanced at her. "That little boy in South Dakota." He shook his head. "I can't get him out of my mind."

"It wasn't your fault."

"Intellectually I know that." He went back to tracing patterns. "But it doesn't stop that look on his face from haunting me. I don't know," he continued. "Maybe I've just seen too much of the dark side of life."

"And your mind's overcrowded with these bad memories—and not enough good ones to balance them?"

He seemed surprised. "Yeah. Maybe."

"So I guess we'll just have to get some good ones in there, huh?" She slid her hands around his neck, slowly pulling his face toward her.

"I guess." The words were muffled against her lips just before he took her mouth in a hungry kiss.

There was going to be a problem. She knew that

as surely as she knew death would someday come. She and Kevin and Jack were traveling down a steep hill, and the end of their journey was predetermined. All that remained to be seen was how long they could delay the inevitable.

As she gave herself up to another hour of afternoon loving, Erica determined to squeeze every bit of goodness she could out of the time she had with Jack. Just as long as she kept in mind that she could lose him at any minute, that she *would* lose him eventually, she'd be able to handle it when she did. She'd be prepared.

And keep Kevin prepared, too.

JACK WAS DOZING when the phone rang. Not sure if Erica was awake, he only shifted as much as he had to in order to get the receiver, holding her against his chest as he did so.

''Shaw,'' he said, reluctant to leave the lethargic peace he'd found in Erica's arms.

''Jack?''

He didn't recognize the voice. ''Yeah?''

''This is Jefferson Cooley.''

Jack sat up, dislodging Erica in the process. Although, technically, he no longer had reason, he felt guilty as hell.

''Hello,'' he said inanely. Did Cooley know that his ex-wife was there with him? Could he somehow have guessed how they'd spent her lunch hour? That would certainly explain the tension in the other man's voice.

"Is Erica there?" Cooley's words were definitely clipped.

"Yes. Just a—"

"No!" Cooley interrupted. "Don't let her know it's me on the phone." Cooley's breathing was rough. "I need your help."

Fully awake now, Jack picked up on the urgency in the other man's tone. "Of course."

"Our son has been taken hostage," Cooley blurted without any attempt at keeping up a facade.

Jack could feel the blood drain from his face. "By whom?" he asked, an automatic calm taking over. "Where and when?"

Erica had been lying there watching him through half-closed lids. He pulled her close, smoothing the hair back from her face, as much to calm himself as to buy her a few more minutes of peace. Just until he had the facts.

"We're not sure of the details," Cooley said. "They noticed him missing from school at recess, but it looks as though he left there of his own free will. A reporter saw him at a Terratruce rally on Capitol Hill. I've been in a meeting, and when the school couldn't find Erica they notified the police. I just got back to my office to find the FBI waiting for me." There was a pause. "They said you were the best," he said simply.

Jack hadn't worked on a missing person's in a

long time. He'd always been better at talking down than he'd ever been at tracking down.

"I'll come immediately," he said, still holding Erica. He was going to have to tell her. "But Rick Charles is the best at finding—"

"Charles is already at work trying to locate Kevin," Cooley said. "They know who has him and they want you ready to go to work."

Understanding what that meant, Jack couldn't tear his mind away from the woman lying against him. This was going to kill her. "How do they know?"

"There's been contact. I've been warned that either I quit fighting the nuclear weapons proposal—or my son dies."

Kevin Cooley had been taken hostage.

ERICA SLID AWAY from Jack even before he'd finished his conversation. She found her panties and bra. Put them on. It had been obvious, just from his side of the conversation, that he was needed.

Probably meant there was a child involved. With her heart in her throat she sent up a silent prayer for the child, that Jack would get there in time, and for the mother—the family—of that child. Wondered how on earth a parent could possibly be expected to cope in a situation like that.

Jack's tension pervaded the air. His face was pinched. In that moment Erica understood why he couldn't think about tomorrows. In the life he'd known all these years, there was only the next hour, the next minute to get people out alive. The days might change, the children might have different names, but to Jack, it all must seem pretty much the same.

He'd told her once that when he was working, there was only one reality. He had to bring that child out alive. His life was going to be worth nothing to him if he didn't.

"Erica." His face pained, he hung up the phone and pulled on the slacks he'd shucked earlier.

"It's okay," she said, wanting to go to him, but knowing she couldn't slow him down. "I'll take care of the lunch trash in the other room and lock up. You just go."

"Erica." The tautness of his voice worried her. He could do this, couldn't he? He'd be able to put South Dakota out of his mind, do the job he'd been trained to do.

"Where are you going?" she asked, trying to keep him focused on the task ahead.

Jack had a core of steel.

"Erica," he said one more time, and grabbed her. "Come here."

He wrapped her so tightly in his arms she could scarcely breathe. But she didn't care. If holding her for a moment would help him, he could hold her any time he wanted.

"Sit with me." He drew her down to the padded bench she'd chosen for the end of his bed. She was still only in panties and bra. Their bare shoulders were touching. "I've got some bad news." He sounded so calm, the words practically slid right off her. "But I want you to know that things are under control. Everything possible is being done, and I promise you that, given the chance, I will not fail this time."

She nodded. "I know you won't." She placed her hand on his thigh. "You go do what you have to do, Jack."

This was what he'd been talking about all along, she suddenly realized, his need to be free to do his job, risk his life, without having someone at home worrying about him. But before she could withdraw the words or say something to reassure him, he spoke again.

"Erica." He laid his hand over hers on his thigh, curling his fingers around it, his palm warming the top of her hand. The way he kept saying her name was starting to bother her. "That was Jefferson on the phone," he said.

"Jefferson who?" The warmth of his hand was in stark contrast to how cold the room had suddenly grown. Shivering, she wondered where her shirt was.

"Your Jefferson. Kevin's been—"

"No!" Jumping up, more defensive than she'd ever been, Erica faced him. And then didn't know what to say. Except "No." She couldn't let him talk to her. Couldn't listen.

Turning, she started to run from the room, from

the apartment, regardless of her state of undress. "Erica!" He grabbed her, held her.

Fighting with all her strength, Erica pummeled his shoulders, pushed against him. "Let me go!" she screamed. "I'm going to get my son from school." The schoolday wasn't over yet, but Kevin would love a free afternoon. Maybe they'd go skating now. They wouldn't even wait for Jack.

He had to work. He'd gotten a phone call.

From Jefferson.

Gulping in air, Erica froze, stared up at Jack. What she read in his eyes took away every ounce of her strength. Her limbs were shaky, too weak to hold her. "Just...no-o-o," she cried, and fell against him, a harsh sob ripping through her.

Jack held her tightly for a couple of seconds, and then sat her away from him, hands on her shoulders. "We've got a job to do, Erica," he said, bending his knees until his gaze was level with hers.

She forced herself to concentrate. To find some composure.

Nodding, she stepped away from him. Where were the rest of her clothes? She had to get dressed. Her slacks were over there. Good. Almost falling, she bent to pick them up, sat on the bed to pull them on, then stood to fasten them. Her shirt. Where was her shirt?

"It's right here," Jack said, holding out the silk shirt she'd dropped so casually on the other side of the bed. He'd finished dressing. Even had on his shoes.

Horrified that she was holding them up, Erica looked down at her pumps, still on the floor with her panty hose.

"Leave the hose," he said, picking up her shoes. "Just put these on."

Jefferson had a cab waiting for them outside. Leading the way, Erica rushed through the apartment, noticing the remains of lunch on the kitchen table, wondering who'd clean it up.

Jefferson. She had to get to Jefferson. He'd…

What? What would he do?

She waited while Jack locked his door behind them and then slid her hand into his as they hurried to the cab. "Tell me," she said.

Whether it was the sunshine on her face, the light of day, she didn't know, but an unnerving calm had come over her, numbing her.

Jack told her everything he'd heard from Jefferson. From a safe, emotionally numb distance she listened, questioned. They had a problem to solve. One step at a time. The first step was gathering the facts. She didn't have to think, just listen.

Didn't have to worry. Or plan ahead. She just had to get through this minute. And then the next. The future didn't exist.

So all the way to the Hart Senate Office Building, where Jefferson and several agents were waiting for her and Jack in a room already cleared and set up as headquarters for the investigation, she listened. And questioned.

And didn't think.

JACK WAITED with them. While he detested the inactivity, he was used to it. They already knew who had Kevin, and as soon as they found out where the boy was being held, he'd go to work. He had to find out as much as he could about the kidnappers, to prepare himself mentally for the job ahead.

And to be there for Erica if she needed him.

She'd walked straight into Jefferson's arms the moment they arrived. And was now sitting with him. Jack understood. They were still very close. And even if they weren't, their missing son was enough to bind them—shared grief providing shared strength.

Still, he desperately wanted to be the one with the right to hold her hand. To hold her up.

Jack stood there, uneasy, as the realization settled over him. He wanted her to need him, trust him, lean on him, the way she did with Jefferson.

The way he and Melissa had done with and for each other.

Turning away from the sight of Jefferson and Erica together, Jack leaned over one end of the conference table and reread the reports that had come in on the alleged kidnappers. They were an extremist right-wing group of college students with some bizarre beliefs—they thought that without a store of nuclear arms as protection, the United States would be wiped out within a year. Jack figured they'd attended an environmental rally to heckle the speakers and generally make trouble. Their leader, Stan Lawson, a senior political-science major, was apparently the man who'd recognized Senator Cooley's son unchaperoned at the Terratruce rally and, seeing an opportunity too good to pass up, had snatched him. It must have happened very quietly. At least two members of Jefferson's staff had been at the rally but they hadn't seen Kevin at all.

"Hi."

Erica came up beside him and Jack straightened. "Hey, babe, how are you doing?" He wanted to pull her into his arms. But he wasn't sure he had that right. Not here. Or now. Not in this part of her life.

"Oh, Jack," she said, her eyes filled with panic as she gazed up at him. She was still the strong capable woman she'd been since walking in the door—but just her awareness of the situation had increased.

Motioning to an agent manning the phones, Jack placed a sheltering arm around Erica's shoulders and led her outside the room to a secluded alcove in the hall.

And then he did what he'd been needing to do since they'd arrived. He held her.

Erica's son—that uncommonly clever, endearing little guy who'd worked so hard to be the perfect host to Jack the night before, to do everything he could to make Jack like him—was now a victim. His daughter had been a victim, too....

Laying his cheek lightly against Erica's, he whispered promises he wasn't sure he'd have the chance to keep. And hardly noticed when her tears mingled with some of his own.

CHAPTER SEVENTEEN

TORN BETWEEN two lovers. Erica supposed that was how it looked to the various personnel in that makeshift headquarters. It was almost eight hours since Kevin had been kidnapped. Concerned colleagues had come and gone, and friends were staffing the phones just to have something to do, to stay close. Sometime during the intervening hours, Jefferson and Jack had established an unspoken truce. They were all in this together—one team with one goal. Get Kevin safely home.

And it felt as if there was a very definite corollary to that. Give Erica the love and support she needed to keep her sane and standing.

In that goal, they'd partially succeeded. She was still standing.

Jack had left the room a little while ago, gone to a smaller room to meet with the mother of the young man who allegedly had Kevin. Trying not to lose all touch with reality, Erica paced the long office they'd been given, moving from the couch to the table where several people sat with phones that had been brought in. From the phones to the conference table spread with reports, pictures and charts. Then over to another table set up with water, coffee, and finger foods that were getting stale. She didn't look out the window, couldn't bear to see the darkness that had settled, to know Kevin was out there somewhere.

She studied the textured wheat pattern in the beige wallpaper, the squares and triangles in the carpet design. The wrinkles in Jefferson's shirt. A smudge on the glass of the coffee table. An ink stain on an agent's shirt pocket. She should know the agent's names by now. She didn't.

There were two women; they'd both tried to speak with her, comfort her. And many men in and out. Members of the Washington police were there. And someone from Georgetown University campus security. And for the past several hours, Pamela. She'd been answering phones, sticking pins in maps when officers and agents called in reporting from different areas. She'd also brought the food that no one, including herself, was touching.

Everything happened around Erica. She was removed from it all, safe in a fog that protected her from the harshest realities.

"They're going to find him." Jefferson had come up behind her.

Arms wrapped around herself, she nodded, staring at a generic floral print on the wall beside the window. Anything to avoid that window, which seemed to continually draw Jefferson to it. Kevin was out there in that darkness.

"Alive," her ex-husband asserted.

Erica glanced at him and nodded again. For most of her life Jefferson had been a strength to her. No matter what the future held for them, she was always going to need him.

"Can we talk for a few minutes?" he asked, gesturing to the couch at the end of the room away from the investigation.

Too overburdened to say much, Erica led the way to the couch, grateful when he sat down right next to her, rather than a seat away. He leaned forward, a common position for him, forearms resting on his knees. In the past couple of years Jefferson's back had started to bother him a lot more—the consequence of a forty-year-old football injury—and leaning forward seemed to take pressure off the lower portion of his spine, easing the pain.

Without thinking, Erica reached over and started to massage his back. She was rewarded with a deeply tired though appreciative smile.

Several minutes passed, filled with the silent communication of two people who knew each other intimately. Erica tried to comfort him and derived a comfort herself from his solid steady presence.

"You need to tell Jack that Kevin is his son."

Her hand froze on his spine. *Kevin.* Just hearing her little boy's name was enough to unhinge her. She'd been trying so hard to concentrate on what was being done—rather than on what hadn't been done yet. Trying to think about the moment in which she found herself, not the moments Kevin might be experiencing. If those men hurt her son, she'd kill them.

"He's going to be negotiating for Kev's release," Jeff continued softly. Every muscle in Erica's exhausted body tensed.

There would be a negotiation. The FBI would find their son. Jack would bring Kevin home to her.

Her little boy hadn't even used his new skates yet.

"He deserves to know." Head turned sideways, Jefferson was looking at her, his gaze unbending and deadly serious.

"No." Tell Jack about Kevin? Put Jefferson through more pain than they were already experiencing? Cause him to lose his son twice in one day? She couldn't fathom such a thing.

She couldn't do it to Jack, either. How much worse would this be for him if he knew the child in danger was his own?

"Yes."

Rubbing his back vigorously, Erica shook her head, refusing to hold his gaze, to let him convince her. "I'm not doing that to you," she said. "Especially not now. In all the ways that matter, Kevin is your son."

He reached behind him and grabbed her hand, then brought it over to hold between both of his. "I love you for that," he said, "for your loyalty to me—"

"Loyalty?"

Jefferson amazed her. Here he was having to spend the most difficult hours of his life in the same room as Jack Shaw. The man his wife had had an affair with. Had borne a child with. And he was still generous enough to see good in her.

"You've always been loyal, Erica. You just happen to be human, as well. The passion you felt for Jack Shaw six years ago wasn't something you chose for yourself, or went out looking for. It was there all along, banked inside you, waiting for the right person to come along." For all the softness of his voice, his words were not gentle, nor did his tone leave room for discussion. "And I knew that."

It was odd how Jefferson glanced toward Pamela then. Reminding himself of a conversation he'd had with her? Drawing strength? Checking to see if she'd seen him there alone with Erica, seen how close they were sitting, seen Erica touching him? Trying to find out if she was angry?

His eyes, when they met Erica's, were sharp with conviction, yet tired, too. It was the first time he'd ever looked old to her. "I knew when I asked you to marry me that there was passion in you," he said. "I knew it wasn't something I was ever going to awaken. I knew it wasn't fair for me to marry you. But I did so, anyway. I was the one who was disloyal, my dear." His voice was low but unfaltering. "You trusted me and I betrayed that trust by talking you into something your heart knew wasn't right."

"You spent every day of our lives together trying to make me happy!"

"And in the meantime, I created a situation that blew up on us. On you most of all."

"How can you say that? You're the one who had to watch your wife grow large with another man's child. And after he was born, you accepted the responsibility of raising him. No child has had a better father than you've been to Kevin."

"And every day for the past five years I've watched the guilt eat you alive."

"I made a wrong choice. I have to be accountable for that."

"If there was anything to be accountable for, it's done," Jefferson said with unyielding authority. "You've proven yourself over time. All these years you've been loyal to me, to Kevin. Even now, with Jack in your life and me out of it, you've remained loyal."

"Because it's right."

"Maybe it was," he allowed. "But you've paid your dues. More than your dues. You've given far more than your loyalty, Erica. You've given me your love, and that's something I will cherish until the day I die."

"It's far less than you've given me." The pain just wouldn't stop. Nor did the pressure of unshed tears. "Even after I was unfaithful to you, you loved me. You didn't leave me, blast me with anger, hate me—all of which I deserved and more. You kept on loving me."

"Because your affair with Jack Shaw was as much my fault as anybody's."

Erica didn't know what to say. Except, "No, it wasn't."

Glancing over, Erica saw Pamela watching them, but while the older woman's face was lined with emotion, Erica sensed support.

"You have to tell him, Erica. He needs to know whose child he's going after."

"Jack rescues every child as if it were his own."

"If you don't tell him, I will."

"It'll make his job much too hard!"

"Erica—"

"What about Kevin?" she interrupted. "He's going to need more stability than ever when we bring him home. It would be cruel to throw this at him right now."

Jefferson sat back and pinned her with one of his most demanding stares. It wasn't a look she'd often been the recipient of. "That young man needs a talking to," Jeff said. "He broke every rule he's ever been given by leaving his school and putting us all— and especially himself—through all this. Forget what Dr. Miller says. There will be no more pandering to his desire to be a grown-up. When he gets home, he's going to be a five-year-old boy. That's it. And for starters, I'm throwing his ties away."

Erica smiled. Somehow Jefferson's speech was exactly what she'd needed to give her flagging strength—and hope—a new boost. Kevin would be back. He wouldn't dare disobey his father.

"You trust Jack with your heart," Jefferson said, his tone more beguiling than autocratic now. "You can certainly trust him with your son's. *His* son's. I've been watching him today, Erica. He's a remarkable man. The kind of man you don't come across very often.

"Of course, I've known that since the beginning. You wouldn't have fallen in love with him otherwise."

"I don't trust him with *my* heart...."

Jefferson glared at her. "Are you going to tell him or am I?"

"But—"

"He won't do anything to hurt Kev, you know that. If it's best that we keep this secret for a while, then we'll do so, but there's something else you need to consider here."

His grim expression scared her. "What?"

"These maniacs want Kevin because he's my son."

Her eyes widened as she sensed where he was heading. "But he isn't."

Oh, God, no. She *was* going to have to tell Jack. The knowledge might help him save Kevin's life.

She thought of what the press would do with this. Of Rudy Wallace. She'd known it was going to come out eventually. She just hadn't expected her time to run out so soon.

Sick to her stomach, she looked at Jeff, hoping he'd have something else to say, some solution other than the one he'd been so adamantly pushing.

The walls were closing in on her. The one thing she'd counted on in her relationship with Jack was retaining the ability to make her own personal choices. She was beginning to understand that you couldn't retain what you'd never had.

"I'll tell him," she whispered.

JEFFERSON TOLD ERICA to use his office to speak with Jack. He'd buzz his private line if Jack's call to move came through. And as he watched them leave the room, her beautiful body supported by an arm bigger, stronger, younger than his own, he was able to do what he'd been trying to do for the better part of a year, something he should've done years before. He said goodbye.

He wished he could have done so without regret. Without second guesses and *if only*s.

Ruefully acknowledging that a small part of him would probably always hate Jack Shaw, he also felt intensely grateful and beholden to the other man. Erica would be well loved.

If they could get through these next hours.

As the door closed behind them, Jefferson knew that one phase of his life had truly ended. And then, just as naturally as his heart mourned the wife he'd loved so completely, he sought out the woman who'd become his lover in every sense of the word.

Her back to him, Pamela was standing by the window, looking out into the night, a cup of coffee cradled between her palms. She saw his reflection in the dark glass and turned toward him. Her smile held not only welcome, but compassion and acceptance.

"You okay?" she asked.

"With that?" He pointed at the door through which Erica and Jack had just disappeared.

Pamela nodded, her gray hair and lively blue eyes such a contrast. One that fascinated him.

"Yes," he said. And with that one simple word, a heavy and very old weight left his shoulders. "I'm fine." Never had he been more grateful to speak the truth.

"I don't know how she's managed to hold it together so well."

"She's an impressive woman."

"And one who loves you very much," Pamela said gently, and only then did Jefferson hear a note of insecurity in her voice.

"As she loved her father, maybe." He said, an arm around the woman he wanted to spend the rest of his life with. "You know, this terrible situation has brought home to me how little control we have over the time left to us," he said. "I don't want to waste a second of whatever allotment that is."

Chuckling, Pamela leaned into him and said, "Senator, I don't think you have a single thing to worry about there. There isn't a man anywhere in the world who can cram more into a day than you do."

"And every minute of that cramming is a waste if I'm not sharing those days with someone I love."

He felt, more than heard, her intake of breath. That, and the fact that she was staring stiffly out into the night, was Jefferson's only indication that his words were having an impact. Pamela always stiffened when things mattered to her.

Jefferson had teased her many times about that reaction, telling her she'd make a terrible poker player. For a brief second he remembered the night she'd allowed him to prove his theory. With her clothes as the ante, he'd very much enjoyed winning that one....

"I'm ashamed it's taken something like this to make me realize it," he said. "Whatever happens here, I want you to know that, for me, you're that someone."

Investigation activity in the room behind them faded, and it sounded to Jefferson as if his words had been shouted through a megaphone. He swallowed, unusually shaky inside. Erica's inability to fall in love with him had done more damage than he'd realized.

He couldn't, in those seconds that he stood there with his confession hanging between them, figure out one single reason Pamela would be pleased to hear it. Or why he'd ever thought she might love him back.

"Did you just tell me that you *love* me?" Her

confident lawyer's voice had disappeared, leaving in its stead a tentative plea.

Her vulnerability gave Jefferson a confidence he hadn't had in many years. "Yes, and," he added, his arm around her, "I want you to marry me."

"You do?"

"Yes."

She turned again to look at him, insecurity clouding her lovely expressive eyes. "Because Erica just walked out that door?"

Jefferson shook his head and pulled her close again, facing her this time. "No," he said, feeling as much conviction in what he was about to say to Pamela as he'd felt in speaking with Erica. "Because I need you with me. Tonight. Right now. Because when I heard about Kevin—" he stopped, swallowed as tears rose to the surface "—I needed *you*. And the minute you walked in that door, today, I had more strength, more courage, than I'd had before you arrived. Because I'm a sixty-five-year-old man facing what might be the worst night of my life and I can't imagine getting through it without you."

Pamela's lips trembled and tears filled her eyes. It wasn't something he'd seen before. She was always so capable, so in control.

"Thank God," she whispered.

"Does that mean you'll marry me?" Some said he was one of the most powerful men in the country, but at that moment he was completely defenseless.

"Yes."

The tension seeped out of him. His arm still around the woman who'd saved him, Jefferson turned with her to look out into the darkness that was concealing his son. There would be time for celebrating later. Time for passion.

Tonight, it was enough that they had each other.

And the ability to pray.

As HE WALKED beside Erica through the building in which she spent so much of her life, Jack could only imagine the hell she must be going through. She held herself rigidly, unnaturally. It almost seemed to him that if he brushed against her, she'd attack. Her steps were deliberate. Staccato.

Concentrating on her kept his thoughts away from the boy who was counting on them to save him.

"Is there some reason in particular that we need to go to Jefferson's office?" he asked.

"No," she said without slowing her stride. Then she shrugged helplessly. "Yes…I don't know. Let's hurry. If they need to reach us, they're going to call on Jeff's private line."

"They also have my cell-phone number," he told her. Jack wouldn't have moved five feet away from the phones all night if he hadn't had that connection.

Pushing the elevator button, Erica stood, neck craned at an uncomfortable angle as she waited for their floor to light up. She stomped her foot once. And then again.

"Come on!" she muttered.

If they didn't find a way to ease her tension soon, she was going to explode. Or fall apart.

Jack didn't like either option.

So he went to work. "Tell me about Kevin."

Avoiding talk of the boy seemed pointless. She'd be torturing herself with thoughts of him, anyway.

Erica's head jerked toward him, her gaze burning him as though he'd lost his mind. "What do you want to know?" she asked sharply, stepping into the open elevator and pushing the button for the right floor.

"Anything that'll help me calm him when I get within speaking distance."

"Until six months ago his favorite things were Power Rangers and baseball. He loved video games—Mario Kart was his favorite. And chocolate milk." Her shoulders started to shake. "He loves chocolate milk."

She broke off, taking long heavy breaths.

It wasn't until they were in Jefferson's office—until he saw the resolute, determined and pitying look on Erica's face—that he realized there was something going on that he knew absolutely nothing about.

CHAPTER EIGHTEEN

ERICA SEEMED very determined to have everything just right as they entered the room. She checked first for messages. When there were none on Jefferson's voice mail, she phoned downstairs to see if they'd missed any news.

He knew they hadn't when her face fell. Moving the phone within reach of the couch, she flicked off the overhead light, turned on some lamps, adjusting their positions on the tables. She closed the curtains. Removed a stack of magazines from the coffee table. Got them both bottles of water from the small refrigerator at the far end of Jefferson's office.

Finally, when Jack was ready to grab her and pin her down, she motioned for him to sit on the maroon leather couch and joined him there.

"We have something we need to discuss." Her preamble did nothing to calm the dread slowly building within him.

She was reconciling with her ex-husband. He'd seen it happen many times. A traumatic event healed rifts in families. In marriages.

Jack knew he and Erica hadn't promised forever.

He'd wanted it that way. He didn't want it that way anymore. Not if it meant he had to lose her.

Yet, wasn't he supposed to have maintained a measure of control here by not allowing himself to make—or accept—any promises?

Head bowed, Erica clasped both hands between her legs. "I...Jefferson said I had to..." She glanced up.

What? Just say it. His inherent patience seemed to have deserted him.

"I can't do this."

Bracing himself, Jack practiced the calming exercises he'd honed to perfection over the years. "When you have something to say, the best way is just to say it."

Jack almost groaned in disgust at the inane remark. He, who was a master at saying the right thing at the right time, talking people down in the most extreme circumstances, sat there sputtering clichés.

He began to hope the phone would ring before Erica had a chance to impart her news. He could get out of there. Get her son back. And get on with his life. The solo life he'd mapped out when—

"Six years ago," she said abruptly, "when we were together in New York..."

"Yeah?"

"We...there were repercussions."

"Jefferson finding out, you mean."

"Well, yeah, but no."

Jack wanted to touch her, needed to, but was afraid

to try. From the moment they'd come to this room, the territory had been foreign, not just the physical space, but the energy between them. Erica was shutting him out.

With no idea where this was going, Jack was forced to sit and wait. No matter how much practice he had at that particular skill, it never seemed to get any easier.

"Jack, Kevin isn't Jefferson's son."

Confused, not sure what Kevin had to do with her and Jefferson getting back together, Jack waited some more.

Erica wrung her hands, clearly not feeling any better after that disjointed statement.

"He thought, in light of the fact that the reason these assholes have my son is because they think he's Jefferson's son, too, I should tell you the truth." She was talking too fast. "We thought the information might make a difference when you go talk to them...."

Jack frowned, his face cold while the rest of his body felt too hot. "Let me get this straight. You're telling me the senator isn't Kevin's father so that I have something to use with the kidnappers. This is a strategy the two of you came up with?"

"Yes," she said. Her eyes were brimming with the oddest combination of emotions. Vulnerability. Stark fear. And pity. "I mean no."

Her eyes pleaded with him to understand. He didn't. Which was it?

"Yes, we wanted you to know because it might make a difference, but no, it's not just a strategy. It's true. Jeff isn't Kevin's father."

"Then who is?" It was the next logical question.

The look on Erica's face was enough to send Jack running from the room. He paled. Thought he'd jumped up from the couch until he found himself still sitting there.

"Who is?" The question was clipped. Cold. She'd better not say what he was deathly afraid she was going to say.

If she did, it would kill him. All he could see was her son's dark-blond hair. And, in his mind's eye, a photo of himself on his fourth birthday...

"I'm sorry," she said, eyes glistening with tears that didn't fall.

So was Jack. "Who is his father?" he repeated the question, speaking very slowly. He couldn't feel her closeness. Didn't think he could feel anything.

"You."

Until he heard that word. Then he felt far too much. Terror. Rage.

Sick.

Standing, Jack strode to the door.

"Where are you going?" Erica's tearful cry stopped him. But only briefly.

"To get those bastards," he said. And then he left.

ERICA LOST TRACK of time. She sat on the couch, just staring, all systems on indefinite hold.

She might have stayed that way for hours if Pamela hadn't come and found her. "Jack ran in a little while ago as though the hounds of hell were at his heels," she said, sitting down and pulling Erica's head to her shoulder, as though it was the most natural thing in the world for her to offer such intimate comfort. As Pamela slowly stroked her hair, Erica turned her face, soaking up the soft warmth of the other woman's palm.

This was real. Soft. Good. She was surprised she could still feel such things.

"When he left again just as quickly, Jefferson told me that Jack is Kevin's father," the older woman continued gently. "I hope you don't mind."

With Pamela offering her the only salvation around, how could she mind? What did it really matter, anyway? What did anything matter?

In the space of a single day, she'd lost everyone in the world who meant anything to her. Kevin. Jefferson. And now, Jack.

"Give him time, sweetie," Pamela was saying.

"He left."

"He'll be back."

He wouldn't. Because he couldn't. She knew Jack. He'd save Kevin if he could. And then she'd never see him again.

"Men are strange creatures," Pamela offered, still running her fingers through Erica's hair. "Sometimes, when their emotions get intense, the only way they can deal with them is through aggression. And when that happens to a good man, he takes himself off so that no one gets hurt. Or he finds a way to channel it. I suspect, based on the questions he asked and orders he barked before he took off, that's what Jack's doing. He's gone to find Kevin. And bring him back.''

The words were nothing more than an attempt at comfort, Erica realized. It was a testimony to her extreme desperation that Erica latched on to them, anyway. Finding in them strength to sit up. To give Pamela a hug. And then, hand in hand with the woman who'd done for Jefferson what Erica had never been able to do, she went back downstairs to face her life.

IT WAS ALMOST one o'clock in the morning when the call came. Kevin was being held inside a boarded-up gas station on the outskirts of the city. Jack was already there. He'd been riding with Rick Charles, the investigative officer in charge, when they'd found him. He was already at work.

It only took Erica a couple of minutes to convince everyone around her that she was going to that gas station. She'd stay out of the way. She wouldn't do anything to hinder Jack or the various officers. But she was going there. No matter what.

Jack was at the back of the garage when the FBI agent pulled up and let Erica and Jefferson out of his car. The front of the station was teeming with men—

several in full body suits with masks. Most of them were standing around, waiting.

As badly as she wanted to be with Jack, to know what was happening, Erica joined the waiting throng. It was a cold night for the beginning of October, and she wasn't dressed for it—especially with her legs bare. She wished she had more than her suit jacket to cover her. But she didn't think anything would really be able to chase away the chill that had settled inside and around her.

The report came that Kevin was alive. His captors had made him speak to Jack to prove it, since he was, after all, their ace.

"Quite a little guy you have there, sir, ma'am," the officer who'd hurried over with the report said to her as she stood with Jefferson. "Apparently no tears at all. He just asked Shaw to do a good job."

Emotion welled up inside Erica, consuming her. With barely a nod, she stared at the station—dry-eyed.

She stood there on the gravel for an hour, her feet swollen and numb in their high-heeled shoes, listening, watching every movement, trying to determine what was going on by the body language of the men poised for action. Though she and Jeff spoke—an occasional observation or question—his presence was a great comfort to her. Much of the time he held her hand.

He and Pamela had told her earlier in the evening that they were getting married.

Had Erica been able to feel anything at all, she'd have been genuinely happy for them. She knew, too, that if her heart survived, she was going to be incredibly relieved. Jefferson deserved to be passionately and completely loved. She'd tried and hadn't been able to feel what she'd wanted to feel.

She'd been standing there so long she almost missed the flurry of activity that started in the corner of the yard. Men were closing in on the building, righting masks that had been shoved back on their heads, raising guns and aiming them at the front door of the station.

They were all watching the corner of the building, and stiffened in readiness when a figure came into view.

Jack.

Crushing disappointment nearly knocked Erica over when she saw he was alone. His eyes scanned the crowd, seemed to settle on her, and then he turned away, speaking with one of the uniformed officers closest to him.

"He wouldn't just be standing there like that if something had happened to Kevin, would he?" she asked Jeff, her teeth chattering.

"Nothing's happened to Kevin." Jeff's voice was strong and sure. "Otherwise those guys would be all over that place."

"Ma'am?" Erica turned to see the officer Jack had been speaking to a moment ago now standing beside her.

"Mr. Shaw has asked if you can come over."

Seeing Jefferson nod, Erica went immediately, her frozen feet carrying her across the gravel at a run.

She didn't know what to expect as she approached Jack. In that setting, as the boss all the officers and agents were looking to for direction, he was intimidating. Frightening in his strength and confidence.

And judging from the way he'd left her that evening, he was furious with her.

As soon as he saw her, he pulled her into his arms. "I've been thinking about you," he said in her ear. The embrace was so quick she could easily have been convinced that she'd imagined the whole thing.

"Lawson has agreed to let Kevin go," he told her, his attention focused on the front door of the abandoned station.

"I didn't have to tell him that Jefferson isn't Kevin's father—which is a damn good thing because that's not something Kevin needed to hear. Lawson's in way over his head and giving himself up. I want you here when Kevin comes out. He's going to be exhausted and frightened and needing his mother."

Trembling, trying not to cry—and not quite succeeding—Erica nodded. She didn't dare hope it was really almost over and yet couldn't stop staring at that door. She had no idea how Jack had created this miracle. Had no idea about anything except that she couldn't breathe until she saw her son again.

The door opened slowly. Every one of the guns around her moved into position.

And then, as though he was simply leaving his school, Kevin came walking out of the building, his feet steady, head held high. It didn't take him long to spot her. Erica knelt down, ready to catch him in her arms as he started to run.

Except that it wasn't his mother he ran to. Instead, he barreled into the strong man standing silently beside her, wrapping his arms around Jack's legs. "Thanks, Jack," he said, looking up, his expression solemn. "I knew you could do it."

Erica was never going to forget the moment she saw her courageous lover grab up that small body in a tight hug. A father's hug.

"Jack?" Kevin asked, pulling back as far as his father would allow. "It's okay, Jack, I'm fine." He finished his assurance with a pat on Jack's cheek.

"I can see that," Jack managed, smiling even while intense emotions played across his face. "I'm glad."

"Hi, Mom." Kevin seemed to have just noticed her. "I guess I'm in trouble, huh?"

"You can count on it, little man." Erica swung around as Jefferson came hurrying up behind her.

"Okay," Kevin said, looking with resignation from one parent to the other. "But do you think I can have a hug first?"

With obvious reluctance Jack released his son, but kept his arm around Erica as she buried her face in Kevin's neck, the tears she could no longer hold back wetting her son's skin. Jefferson took him next, giving the boy a hug, then chastising him and telling him—at virtually the same time—how very much he was loved. He handed him back to his mother, who held him tightly.

His gaze moving between all three adults, Kevin reached out very dirty fingers to wipe tears off their faces. "It's okay, you guys," he said. "I cried a lot, too, at first, but it goes away."

LAWSON AND THE OTHER students were taken into custody, business was wrapped up, and Kevin had to be fed, bathed and put to bed. Because Jefferson wanted to swing by the Hart Senate Office Building and pick up Pamela, Jack offered to ride with Erica and Kevin in the back of Agent Charles's car to Erica's condo.

For someone who had babbled almost nonstop all the way home, his little legs bouncing on the seat, Kevin was noticeably subdued as the four adults in his life fussed around him once they had him home. Needing to be everywhere at once, Erica stopped in the kitchen to make suggestions to Pamela about what to make for Kevin to eat—in spite of the fact that Jefferson's fiancé already had Kevin's favorite— boxed macaroni and cheese—going on the stove. In Kevin's bedroom she turned down his covers, collected fresh underpants and the Power Ranger pajamas tucked under his pillow, stopping to plug in his night-light on her way out.

And then she ran into Jefferson and Jack in the

bathroom. The men were taking turns scolding the poor little guy, subjecting him to far more of a lecture than he needed at that moment as Jefferson helped him with his bath and Jack stood back, watching the proceedings.

"It's almost four o'clock in the morning, you guys. Give him a break," Erica said.

Shooing them out of the way, she bent over the tub to wash Kevin's ears. Her fervent gaze took in every inch of her son's body, because she had to make certain there wasn't so much as a bruise on his tender young skin.

And because it had been a very long day, she didn't fight the stray tear or two that fell into the bath.

JACK HAD TO GET some sleep. It was almost five in the morning and this had been a very long night. Jefferson and Pamela had gone home to bed half an hour before, but would be back soon. No one wanted to be very far from Kevin.

Jack couldn't even seem to leave the boy's room.

Jack sat in a chair across from Kevin's bed and watched the covers move as the little guy breathed. Watched and counted. Watched and counted. He found a measure of calm in Kevin's steady breathing.

He could find no calm anywhere else.

"I used to do that." Erica's soft voice came from the doorway.

He hadn't known she was there. Didn't look at her

now. One, two, three, four. Kevin took about four breaths every ten seconds.

"When he was first born, I was afraid he'd die if I left him alone in his crib....."

"Sudden Infant Death Syndrome." Melissa had worried about Courtney, too.

"Sometimes at night I'd sit in here for hours, watching him breathe and thinking about you."

Jack didn't want to hear that. Didn't want any of it. Love. Commitment. People in his life who mattered more than life itself. Vulnerability. Things he couldn't control. Being alone. Walking away. Emptiness.

Turning his head slowly, he looked at her.

"You want to talk?" she asked.

He didn't. He got up, anyway. Followed her into the den. He liked this room most of all. Liked the wall of windows that gave him the illusion of being able to see the whole world. Made him feel as if he was in control of *something*.

When, in actuality, he was in control of nothing at all.

Erica came up behind him, wrapped her arms around him, laid her head on his back between his shoulder blades. She was trembling. "Thank you."

He nodded.

"I'm sorry."

He nodded again.

"Say something."

"I don't know what to say." Dawn was going to

be breaking soon. Jack was sorry to see the darkness fade. He wasn't ready for the light of day.

With one last squeeze, she let go and came around to stand beside him. "Are you angry?"

"I think so, yeah."

"At me?"

He couldn't figure that out. "No." But he continued, "I lost five years of my son's life."

She didn't say anything, just slid her hand into his. He let her hang on. Eventually his fingers took hold of hers. Her words of a few moments ago kept playing through his mind. Maybe because here and now was all he could handle.

"Thank you," he said.

"For what?"

"Having him. Doing such a great job raising him. Loving him." All things he should have shared with her. Taken responsibility for. Risked.

"He's easy to love."

Jack could already tell that. Which brought its own shot of panic. And regret. He'd lost so much. All these years, he'd been traveling around alone, living alone, existing alone. Mourning the wife and daughter he'd lost. And all that time he'd had a son.

It took every bit of strength he had to contain the rage. He wasn't even sure what brought it on. The loss? The regret? The fact that she hadn't given him a choice? That even now, his choices had been taken from him? Every day for the rest of his life was going to be filled with the knowledge that the incredible agony of losing Courtney could happen all over again.

"I have a son."

"Yes."

"Mine." He couldn't quite grasp it.

"Yes."

"That little man who marched out of there tonight, so confident that his world was going to be okay, is my son." Tears burned the back of his eyes, scaring him. Before that night, he hadn't cried in years.

"Yes."

Despite himself, the tears rolled down his face, dripped off his chin. The skyline blurred until nothing had shape or definition. There was only color.

He felt a tug on his hand and was too beaten to fight it. He ended up on the couch, in Erica's arms, her gentle hands soothing him. Years of grief, of fear, broke free. Tears for Melissa. And baby Courtney. For Erica and the torment these years must have been. Tears for Jefferson Cooley, a man whose only sin was that he'd loved too much. Tears of loneliness. For lost years, missed opportunity. Everything that had been building came rushing to the surface and he was powerless to stop it.

And now there was more—something he'd promised himself he'd never live with again. *Fear*. Cold, all-consuming fear.

At the moment Jack preferred the loneliness.

KEVIN MIGHT HAVE GAINED a father—the operative word being *might*—but Erica knew she'd lost a lover. Jack's withdrawal was tangible.

The worst part was, she understood. If she'd learned nothing else through all of this, she'd learned that no amount of determination or hard work could force feelings. And that it took more than love to build bridges. She'd loved Jefferson, but no amount of trying had been able to make her fall in love with him. Or arouse passion where there was none.

In the same way, Jack might love her, might grow to love Kevin, but no amount of determination would be enough to overcome the fear that drove him away. No amount of love could turn back time and reverse the loss of Jack's faith in life, or bring back Courtney or Melissa.

Erica didn't know what her future held, but as she lay there cradling Jack she realized that having him in her life had been an act of fate. Ironically, through all the hell she'd suffered since meeting him, since making the biggest mistake of her life, she'd found peace. Maybe not a peace that would diminish the pain of daily living, the heartache. But a peace that would at least give her the strength to survive it.

"We probably shouldn't tell Kevin about me just yet." Jack's words sounded far too loud, interrupting the long silence that had fallen. "He's had enough trauma for a while."

"Jefferson and I already spoke about that," Erica said carefully. Of course, part of the decision was Jack's now, but she and Jefferson had been raising Kevin on their own for a long time. "We both think that it'll be less traumatic for him if we're straight with him from the beginning, rather than letting him think you're just a friend only to change things later. Besides, it's time Kevin found out that there are many bosses in his life, and he isn't one of them. He needs security, and I think knowing you're his father, knowing that he has not one but two remarkable men fighting his battles, might help Kevin.''

''So when are we going to tell him?''

She'd expected more of a fight. Tried not to read too much into his easy acquiescence.

''In the morning.''

''As in *this* morning? A couple of hours from now?'' Jack asked.

She nodded. ''Don't you think you've lost enough time?''

His lips tightened with deep emotion. Acting purely on instinct, Erica leaned forward and kissed them softly, coaxing him to trust her. To trust himself.

It wasn't a task that could be completed in the short period they had left to them.

KEVIN WOKE UP scared, afraid to open his eyes. And then in his head, he heard Jack's voice, talking to the bad guys who'd taken him from Mr. Terratruce's party.

And remembered that he was safe.

Opening his eyes slowly, he was really, really glad

to see his room. The Power Rangers were there, just like they were supposed to be. And so was he.

He climbed out of bed quietly and sat on the floor. Maybe he could play for a little while before his mom heard him. He could have a little bit of fun before he got in trouble.

It really stank. The bad guys had grabbed him and *he* had to get punished for it. And what stank worst was that he didn't get any work done at the party. He didn't even get to talk to one person or find out one thing about nucl'ar munitions.

Kevin heard voices coming from Mommy's room. And that stank, too. He wouldn't have time to even put on his skates so he could pretend he was skating before she yelled at him. She was probably going to take the new skates away. Or maybe Jack would.

His daddy would for sure if he knew he had them. Daddy had been madder at him than Kevin could ever remember.

But he'd hugged him tight, too. Everything was okay as long as Daddy kept hugging him.

The voices were coming closer to his room. Kevin looked up at his bed, wondering if he had time to get back in there and hide under the covers. Maybe Mommy would think he was asleep.

He got up. Made a run for it. Started climbing into bed.

"We thought we heard you!" Mommy said. His butt was still in the air. Kevin froze, waiting to see how mad she was.

''How you feeling, sport?''

He turned around slowly. He liked it when she called him sport. And she didn't sound the way she usually did when he did something that made her mad.

''Did you sleep well?''

He shrugged, trying to figure out if she was mad at all. She sure didn't look it. And then he noticed Jack there, too. In the same clothes as he had on last night.

Jack didn't seem mad, either.

''We've got something to tell you, okay?''

He nodded. He was probably gonna get it now.

Mommy sat down on the bed and put her arm around him. It was an odd kind of being in trouble. Jack stood in front of them, but his shoulders were all hunched, like he was the one going to get yelled at.

Kevin wondered if maybe he hadn't woken up yet.

''Where's Daddy?'' he asked. Daddy was the one who was going to be the maddest.

''He'll be here soon,'' Mommy said. Her voice was funny, and Kevin suddenly felt worried.

''Am I going to get spanked?'' He'd never been spanked before, but his friend Bobbie had and he said it was the most awful thing. Kevin figured he might get the most awful thing for going to that party.

He wished he'd never heard of the dumb party.

''No, although we're going to have to talk about your rules,'' Mommy said. At least she sounded a little bit more like Mommy. "What we want to talk to you about is something different," she said. She looked up at Jack like she had a question, but then she didn't ask it.

"Before you were born, I knew Jack," Mommy said. "And I loved him."

Kevin nodded. That was okay.

"And when two people love each other, sometimes they make a baby."

Bobbie had told him that once and Kevin had hit him. "That's gross. Do I have to know about it?"

"This time you do because it's important. Because Jack and I made a baby back then."

"Where is it?"

"Right here. You are the baby we made."

Kevin didn't get it. "I'm not a baby."

"No, but you were," Mommy said. "You've seen the pictures."

"That was a long time ago." He looked up at Jack. "You made me?" he asked.

Jack nodded.

"I thought daddies made kids."

Jack nodded again.

"So you're my daddy, too?"

"Yes, son, I am."

Wow. This was the best trouble he'd ever been in.

"Do you know what to do about nucl'ar munitions?" Kevin asked. Jack sure seemed to know everything else.

"I'll make a deal with you," Jack said. "You concentrate on following your rules and letting the adults take care of you, and your father and I'll worry about nuclear weapons. Deal?''

''Deal.'' Kevin figured he had to be the luckiest guy around. When Bobbie got in trouble, he got spanked. When Kevin did, he got another dad.

''So now I got two dads?'' he asked, just to make sure.

Jack and Mommy looked at each other, kinda smiling, but Mommy seemed like she was gonna cry, too. Kevin got scared. He hoped he hadn't just messed everything up.

''Yes, sport, you've got two dads,'' she said, and Kevin felt good again. ''Is that okay with you?''

'''Course,'' Kevin said, jumping down from the bed. ''Do you think we can go skating today?'' he asked hesitantly, moving over to study his new skates.

''I think that can be arranged,'' Mommy said. ''Missing a day of school won't be the end of the world.''

Mommy and Jack picked him up at once and hugged him between them. He felt better than he had in a long, long time.

''Like a sandwich,'' he said. ''A Kevin sandwich.''

Mommy and Jack laughed.

''Hey,'' Kevin said, thinking of all the things he had to tell Bobbie. And the thing Bobbie was going to ask him. ''Do I get to call you Daddy, too?'' He wrinkled his brow in puzzlement. "'Course Daddy's already Daddy, but you could be Dad."

Bobbie wouldn't think Jack was really his daddy if he had to call him Jack.

"Just to make sure I always answer you, it would be best if you did," Jack said matter-of-factly.

Kevin grinned. "Okay, Dad!"

And that was when he knew for sure that the bad times were over.

He'd been sad and scared for a long time. But now he was going to get to play ball again.

He hoped.

JACK DIDN'T MAKE LOVE to her anymore. Hadn't since the night he'd become a dad. It had been three weeks and he hadn't so much as kissed her. Until then, Erica hadn't known it was possible to feel so happy and so incredibly heartbroken at the same time.

Kevin had a new dad. And Jack had a son.

He just didn't seem capable of taking on any more than that. The risk was too great. He'd been pushed too far.

It was the most difficult thing in the world for Erica to realize that she'd finally come up against a problem she couldn't fix. No matter how hard she tried, how much she did, how diligently she worked, she had no effect on Jack. His heart was completely outside her circle of influence.

Why that came as a surprise, she didn't know. His

heart had never been hers. She knew that. Their relationship had worked because they'd kept their hearts to themselves.

At least, *he* had. She amended that last thought. Somehow, over the past weeks, Jefferson's words had filtered through her, and she now recognized their truth. He'd said months ago that she was in love with Jack. Said that night in New York would not have happened if she hadn't been.

Seeing Jack face his fears enough to embrace Kevin had made her take a long look at herself. And what she saw was that, once again, her ex-husband had been right. Denying her love for Jack, allowing it to be obscured by fear, did not mean it didn't exist.

It only meant she wasn't embracing it.

Sitting on the front step of her condo, dressed only in jeans and a sweater in deference to Washington's Indian summer, she watched as Jack hunkered down next to Kevin by a small mound of sand on the grass. Identical blond heads were almost touching as they peered at a bullet-shaped metal cylinder half-buried in the middle of the sand.

Father and son were dressed almost identically in jeans, long-sleeved FBI T-shirts and white running shoes.

"Okay," Jack said. "You saw how we mixed the food coloring and the baking soda."

His hand on Jack's knee for balance, Kevin nodded. "And we let it dry enough, I'm sure about that, Dad."

"I trust you, Kevin."

"Is it really gonna explode, just like it was a nucl'ar bomb?"

"I think so." Jack was intent on the boy and the experiment in front of them.

Erica watched her son and his father, her heart full—and oh, so lonely, too. She was sitting there glimpsing perfection. As it might have been in another place, another time. Jack hadn't glanced at her once.

"Before we pour in the vinegar, I want you to tell me once more why we're doing this."

"Well, just like the vinegar's going to make the soda explode and put the colors up, the chemicals in nucl'ar bombs send vapors in the air…"

"And?"

Kevin frowned. "And after I get to see the vapors so I'll know what a bomb sorta looks like, I'm not allowed to think about nucl'ar munitions anymore, 'cause it's a grown-up job."

"You made a promise, son."

"I know."

"And you understand what it means?"

Tears burned the back of Erica's eyes as her son nodded solemnly. "I promise not to worry 'bout nucl'ar bombs anymore, and to follow all the rules, no matter what."

"Good." Jack nodded just as solemnly. "You sure you're ready to keep that promise?"

Jack had been working diligently with the little boy for three weeks, talking with him every day, reasoning, reassuring, laughing, making games—all culminating in this ritual now, with the make-believe bomb as a symbolic send-off to Kevin's obsession.

"I'm sure."

"Then pour in the vinegar and the promise is made."

Carefully, slowly, Kevin picked up the little cup of vinegar, placing it near the lip of the spout sticking up from the metal cylinder. He hesitated, looked at Jack.

"Will you make a promise, too, Dad?"

"What's that?"

"Will you promise always to be my dad and not go away?"

"For as long as I'm alive."

"Then shouldn't you have your hand on the vinegar, too?"

Blinking back her tears, Erica smiled. Her son was one smart little boy.

"I guess I should," she heard Jack say.

With the strong male hand on top of the small one, the two guys she loved tipped their cup.

The air filled with a mushroom of colorful vapors that sealed the fates of a little boy and the man who'd fathered him.

And left Erica feeling strangely sad and alone.

FEELING HIS SON'S HAND beneath his, Jack watched the vinegar pour from that cup, and that was when he finally saw the truth.

A five-year-old boy trusted him enough to turn away from his fears. It was time Jack started being at least half the man his small son was.

He'd spent so many years building walls against the pain, he'd forgotten what mattered most. People. Loved ones he could care about, care for, take care of.

He could feel Erica sitting behind him, could almost feel her relief as her little boy released an obsession that had almost cost him his life.

As he heard the hiss of vinegar meeting soda, watched the colorful cloud of vapors rise up, he knew that just as Kevin was letting go, he had to let go, too. He could spend his entire life running from the storm. Or he could stop and find the rainbow. He wouldn't even have to look very hard. It was right there in front of him.

And now he had to do the ultimate talking-down job. To save his own life this time. Erica had taken him hostage. And he had to free himself to love her....

As soon as Kevin had left for Jefferson's—where he'd no doubt give his father and Pamela a detailed and very glowing account of their "bombing" experiment—Jack grabbed Erica's hand.

"Can we talk?" he asked.

He couldn't blame her for seeming startled. Every

other time his visit with Kevin had ended these past weeks, Jack hadn't been able to leave fast enough.

"Sure," Erica said.

"Inside?"

"Okay."

She led the way, took a seat on the leather couch in her den. Though he would've liked to pace to the wall of windows, stare out and think about escape, Jack knew that his running days were over. He sat down next to her.

"That kid who killed Melissa and Courtney," he said with no preamble whatsoever. "I let the bastard rob me of much more than my wife and daughter." Those words on his tongue were a shock, finding their way through pain that had crippled him far too long.

"What more?" Erica asked softly. He hated the reserve in her voice, in her gaze. He'd never found it so difficult to talk to her. Or needed to so badly.

He regretted so much that they'd come to this.

His voice was low and serious. "I was so busy trying to prevent further pain, I actually brought it on myself by refusing to let in the possibility of joy."

She pulled on a little orange thread in the outer seam of her jeans. "I had a similar thought the night Kevin was being held hostage."

"How so?"

"Sitting there all those hours, wondering if I'd ever get to hold my baby again..." Her voice broke, but there was no other indication of the pain he knew she was reliving. "I was thinking about you, about how if we didn't get him out of there, you'd never have the chance to know him. At least I would've had my memories…"

He wanted to hold her in his arms.

"…and then I thought about how much I'd relied on memories of you all these years. When times were toughest and I thought I couldn't endure any more, I'd think of you and know that I could. When I hated myself for being unfaithful to Jefferson, for hurting this man who'd been nothing but good to me, I'd think of the value you'd seen in me and pray that it was still there. I'd vow to make myself the kind of woman you'd thought I was…."

"The kind of woman you are," Jack said fiercely, giving in to his need to pull her against him, relieved as hell when she didn't resist. "You're a miracle, Erica. I've never met anyone who loves as selflessly as you."

"I don't know about that," she said, and when he heard her disbelief, Jack knew that if it took him the rest of his life, he was somehow going to free Erica of the erroneous opinion she had of herself. She was berating herself for the very thing that made her remarkable—her deep love, her loyalty—and he had to make her see how wrong that was.

"But what I do know," she went on, "what these past weeks have shown me, is that you never have control over losing someone you love. Whether it's through infidelity, lack of passion or an act of crime—there's always going to be that risk.''

Jack froze inside until he felt her breath against him, reminding him of everything he'd only recently found. Everything he'd recovered. The warmth of her body gave him the courage to venture further into territory he'd sworn never to inhabit again.

''But the thing is, for every minute you and Melissa had together, you have a memory that will sustain you. The memories are eternal.''

Like a cool breeze against his skin, Jack felt a freedom he hadn't thought he'd ever feel again. With a few simple inspired words, uttered by a woman he'd instinctively known he could trust, Erica was not only giving him hope for a future, she'd given him back his past. She'd given him back Melissa and Courtney.

And he had some giving to do, too. If she'd allow him…

''MARRY ME.''

Jack's chest rumbled with words, but Erica was certain she'd dreamed them. She'd spent far too much time alone with her thoughts lately. Too much time dealing with too much hurt.

''It's the only way.''

''Way for what?'' she asked hesitantly, not sure she understood him.

''It's the only way to make life right.''

''Why?''

"Because I love you so much it makes me crazy. And it's obvious from what you've told me, what you've done, what you've shown me, that you love me, too. I think that surpasses everything else."

She wanted so badly to believe him. But guilt prevented her. It was always there. The price she had to pay. "I put Jefferson before you."

"No. You might've tried, you *had* to try, but you couldn't. It wasn't him you were loving when you sat up in Kevin's room at night. Hell, as hard as you tried, it wasn't him you were loving when you went to bed."

"I didn't tell you about your son."

"We made damn sure that you didn't have a way to contact me."

"I didn't even try."

He shook his head. "Listen to me, Erica. This was a difficult situation, an impossible situation, and you made your decisions intuitively, not analytically. With your heart, not your brain. And your heart told you I wasn't ready to accept what I learned here tonight. So you protected me. And Kevin and Jefferson, too. You gave your son an incredible father. You gave your husband the son he could never have—and an enormous amount of love. And you gave me the space and time I needed to heal."

Could he possibly be talking about *her?* Could she really have done all that?

"The only person you weren't loving," he continued, drawing her up so that their faces were only inches apart, ''was yourself.''

The concept was too incredible to grasp all at once, but Erica held on to it, knowing that she'd come back to it again and again for the rest of her life, trying to be the woman he saw in her. And maybe even to believe that this woman really existed.

''You love selflessly, Erica.'' He leaned his head against the couch, studying her from beneath half-lowered lids. ''Which is why you need someone who'll make sure you get loved, too.''

Erica spent her life coping, not soaring.

''You have to marry me,'' he said, his mouth breaking into a tired yet peaceful grin. ''Either that, or have a five-year-old man bossing you around. That kid's dangerous!''

She grinned back. It was either that or completely humiliate herself by sobbing all over him.

''He has no idea how lucky he is,'' she said. ''Has no idea what an incredible gift you are to his life.''

''*You're* his most incredible gift, Erica,'' Jack said quietly. ''And mine, too.''

''I want to believe that.''

''Say you'll marry me and I'll spend the rest of my life convincing you.''

''Okay.''

''That's a yes?''

''Yes.''

''You're sure?''

''Jack! If you give all your hostage-takers this

much opportunity to change their minds, it's amazing you get anyone out.''

"I only need their agreement for a minute or two. Yours has to last forever.''

He had no idea how glad she was to hear that. "Okay. Yes. I'm sure. Forever…''

They spent the next few hours exploring just how great forever was going to be.

KEVIN WAS PLEASED to see his dad at his house when Daddy dropped him off the next morning. It was Sunday, and that meant maybe they could play and have some fun because it seemed Dad didn't work on Sundays. Not like Daddy had to sometimes.

Mom and Dad were sitting on the couch in the den. They had funny looks on their faces. He went in and wedged himself between them.

"We've got something we want to tell you, Kev. Okay?'' Dad said.

"Sure.'' He bounced his legs on the couch. He liked the squishy sound.

"Jack and I are going to get married,'' Mom said.

"You are?'' Kevin looked up at the man who'd saved him from the bad guys. "Because you saved me?''

"Because we love each other,'' Jack said. "And because we love you, too.''

Kevin frowned, his neck hurting a little from having to look so far sideways. "I'm bad sometimes.''

"Everyone makes mistakes, Kev,'' Dad told him.

"And when you do, you'll be in trouble, but we'll still love you."

He thought that sounded okay.

"Is it all right with you if I marry your mom and live here with you?"

"Does Daddy know?"

"Yes. We talked to him this morning."

"And he said you could?"

"Yes."

"I don't have to share my room, do I?" It wasn't that he didn't *want* to, but his bed was pretty small, and besides, real mommies and dads slept together, and Kevin wanted a real mommy and dad. It scared him when Mommy was in her room all alone and he heard her cry.

If Dad was in there with her, he'd make her feel better.

"No, you don't have to share your room," Dad said, his mouth twisting in kind of a smile even though he sounded serious. "I'll be sharing your mother's room, if that's okay with you."

"Okay. Can we go skating now?"

"You're sure?" Dad asked.

"Yep, I want to go skating."

"I meant about your mom and me getting married."

"Oh. Yeah." Did that mean they didn't get to skate?

"Marriage is a promise, Kevin. It's not something you can change your mind about."

"Jack!" Mommy laughed. "Give it up already!"

"I just want—"

Kevin didn't hear what it was his dad wanted. He'd just had a thought that might be good. And might be horrible. But was probably good.

"Wait a minute," he interrupted Dad. "Does this mean you might make another baby?"

"Would it be okay with you if we did?"

Yeah, it would probably be good. 'Specially since he didn't have to think about nucl'ar weapons anymore.

"Okay, but would I have to share my room?"

Mommy and Dad laughed, and Kevin figured that next time Bobbie had a birthday party, he was going to be catcher.

C'mon back home to Crystal Creek with
a BRAND-NEW anthology from

bestselling authors
Vicki Lewis Thompson
Cathy Gillen Thacker
Bethany Campbell

Return
to
Crystal
Creek

**Nothing much
has changed in
Crystal Creek...
till now!**

The mysterious Nick Belyle has shown up in town,
and what he's up to is anyone's guess. But one
thing is certain. Something big is going down in
Crystal Creek, and folks aren't going to rest till
they find out what the future holds.

*Look for this exciting anthology,
on-sale in July 2002.*

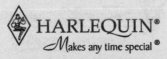

*These New York Times bestselling authors
have created stories to capture the hearts and minds
of women everywhere.
Here are three classic tales about the power of love—
and the wonder of discovering the place
where you belong....*

FINDING HOME

DUNCAN'S BRIDE
by
LINDA HOWARD

CHAIN LIGHTNING
by
ELIZABETH LOWELL

POPCORN AND KISSES
by
KASEY MICHAELS

*Available only from Silhouette
at your favorite retail outlet.*

Where love comes alive™

Visit Silhouette at www.eHarlequin.com

PSFH

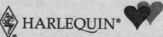

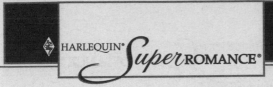

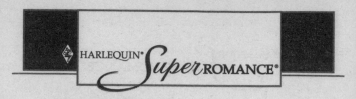

HARLEQUIN *Super* ROMANCE

They'd grown up at Serenity House—a group home
for teenage girls in trouble. Now Paige, Darcy and
Annabelle are coming back for a special reunion,
and each has her own story to tell.

SERENITY HOUSE

An exciting new trilogy
by
Kathryn Shay

Practice Makes Perfect—June 2002
A Place to Belong—Winter 2003
Against All Odds—Spring 2003

Available wherever Harlequin books are sold.

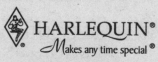

HARLEQUIN®
Makes any time special®